"So how *exactly* … *me about erotica* …

Joan squirmed nervously in her seat. "I was just pondering my lesson plan," she murmured. "I think we'll need to take a hands-on approach. *Very* hands-on."

Her words washed over him like a caress. Bryce slid his hand over hers, twining their fingers. Then he lifted their joined hands and pressed a slow kiss to her fingers. It was time to get their school for scandal under way. "I'm ready for class to begin."

She shivered, a slight tremor that brought him tremendous satisfaction. "Soon," she said, closing her eyes. He brought the tip of one finger into his mouth, his tongue spiraling around her soft skin. Her breath hitched. "Very soon," she whispered.

His teeth grazed lightly over her finger as he slipped the digit free, then pressed a kiss to the inside of her wrist. "Good," he said. "Just so you know, I always ace my classes."

Dear Reader,

When Joan first introduced herself to me in *Silent Confessions,* my latest single-title release, I knew I had to give her a story of her own—particularly one that explored the erotic fantasies Joan discovers daily between the pages of the rare books she works with. But what fun is a fantasy—especially sensual fantasy—without the perfect man to share it? And what man could be more perfect than Bryce Worthington, a sexy-as-sin multimillionaire who's more than willing to take Joan's academic interest in erotica to new and intimate heights?

I had a lot of fun writing Joan's story. She's definitely a dreamer, a woman who believes in happily ever after. But this fairy tale definitely isn't for kids....

I hope you enjoy *Silent Desires.* And if you missed it, be sure to look for *Silent Confessions,* which was available last April.

I love to hear from readers, so please let me know what you think. You can e-mail me at julie@juliekenner.com or write me at P.O. Box 151417, Austin, TX 78715-1417. And please visit my Web site at www.juliekenner.com for contests, news and more.

Happy reading!

Julie

Books by Julie Kenner

HARLEQUIN BLAZE

16—L.A. CONFIDENTIAL

HARLEQUIN TEMPTATION

772—NOBODY DOES IT BETTER
801—RECKLESS
840—INTIMATE FANTASY
893—UNDERCOVER LOVERS

Julie Kenner

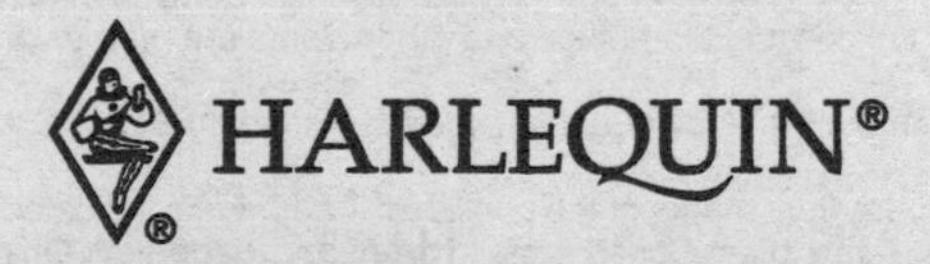

TORONTO • NEW YORK • LONDON
AMSTERDAM • PARIS • SYDNEY • HAMBURG
STOCKHOLM • ATHENS • TOKYO • MILAN • MADRID
PRAGUE • WARSAW • BUDAPEST • AUCKLAND

For Brenda.

ISBN 0-373-79102-X

SILENT DESIRES

This edition published by arrangement with Harlequin Books S.A.

Visit us at www.eHarlequin.com

Printed in U.S.A.

1

THE LITTLE BELL above the door of Archer's Rare Books & Manuscripts jingled as Jack Parker slipped out the door and into the dark. Joan Benetti looked on, amused and, if truth be told, a little sad. After almost a year of marriage, Veronica Archer Parker, her boss and friend, was about to follow her husband out the door and head off on her belated honeymoon.

How cool was that?

Joan sighed. Pretty damn cool, actually. For years, Joan had done the New York singles thing, hopping from bar to bar and guy to guy. It had been a hoot and a half, no doubt about that, but now...well, maybe now it was time to get serious. And not just about a man. About a lot of things. Lately Joan had been using Veronica's life as a mirror, and over and over Joan had found her own reflection wanting.

"Hey?" Veronica—Ronnie, as everyone called her—tapped a fingernail on the glass display counter, her voice pulling Joan from her reverie. "You in there?"

Joan looked up, manufacturing a grin. "Of course. I'm just tired. This four in the morning thing sucks."

Ronnie laughed. ''Can't help it. The plane leaves at six and I needed to grab a few things from the office. But you didn't have to get up.''

Joan yawned, the talk of sleep making her tired all over again. ''I didn't get up. I was already up.'' She was temporarily living in Ronnie's old apartment above the bookstore, so she'd thought she might as well come down when she heard Jack and Ronnie come in for the reference books and notes Ronnie was taking with her to Paris and London. The honeymoon was a working trip, but Jack didn't seem to mind.

''Awake all night,'' Ronnie said, her expression amused. ''And what does this one do?''

Joan rolled her eyes. ''I wasn't with a guy.''

Ronnie's brow furrowed. ''But it's Saturday night. Well, Sunday morning.''

''Yeah? So?'' Joan knew she sounded defensive, but she couldn't help it. Instead of dating, she'd spent the weekend reading and thinking. Big, sweeping life thoughts. ''Who-Am-I and What-Should-I-Do-With-My-Life'' type questions. Ones best pondered in the dark with a Nina Simone CD and a bottle of merlot. Of course, while she was pondering in the dark, she'd missed flirting with Roy, the DJ at Xylo's, and she'd *really* missed the bar's famous chocolate martinis. But, for the most part, she'd enjoyed her weekend alone. Well, okay, so it was only one night alone, but still… She'd made some important decisions, and that was the key.

Ronnie shrugged. "It's no big deal," she said. "I just assumed you'd have a date."

"Yeah, well, I'm on hiatus." Joan grinned, then waved to Jack who'd stepped back inside. Ronnie moved easily into his arms, and Joan felt that little tug at her heart again.

The truth was, it was Ronnie's impending honeymoon that had kick-started Joan's meditative mood. Jack had rolled out the fairy-tale golden coach for Ronnie and he was whisking her off to the ball. And as far as Joan could tell, Ronnie's coach showed no signs of turning back into a pumpkin.

That was the trouble with all of Joan's dates. Trey, Andy, Martin, Jim—and all the rest of them. They were no princes, and no matter how much fun she might have had at the ball with them, the fantasy always came to an end. It sucked, and Joan was tired of it.

"I'm swearing off drive-by dating," Joan blurted, trying her resolution on for size. Ronnie and Jack both looked up, their expressions curious but not too surprised. Okay, so maybe Joan did tend to make a lot of resolutions, but they usually involved diets or exercise. *This* one she intended to keep.

"Swearing off?" Ronnie repeated.

"Well, yeah," Joan said. She lifted her chin, reminding herself why she was doing this. "If it looks like there might be something real there, then sure I'll date. But no more of this random stuff."

"A woman with a plan," Jack said. "I almost feel like I should issue some sort of warning to my poor, unwed brothers in arms."

At that, both Joan and Ronnie rolled their eyes. "We have a taxi waiting," Ronnie said to Jack as she pointed toward the door. "Go make sure the driver doesn't take off with our stuff."

He kissed her. "I'll meet you out there," he said. He paused at the door. "I asked Donovan to drop by now and then. Just to make sure everything's okay."

Joan grinned. Jack was a homicide detective and his partner, Tyler Donovan, was a good guy who looked about ready to tie the knot himself with a nurse he'd been dating steadily for months. Both men tended to be overprotective. Joan pretended to be annoyed, but in truth, their concern made her feel special. "Thanks, Jack," she said, then grinned when his expression of surprise revealed that he'd been expecting a protest.

"You're welcome," he said, and she wondered what argument for her safety and well-being he'd had to toss by the wayside.

Once he was outside again, Ronnie moved back toward the counter. "So you're really giving up dating?"

"Sure. It's no big deal," Joan said.

"Uh-huh." Ronnie didn't look convinced. Which made sense. Joan wasn't certain she was convinced, either. "Are you sure you'll be okay?"

This time, Joan knew she wasn't talking about her dating life, but about running the store. "Fine," she said. "I've been working here four years now. I think I'm getting the hang of it."

Ronnie had the good grace to look a little sheepish. "Still, it's a big responsibility. You've never done the books or payroll before. And it's not like there's a lot of room in the budget." She frowned. "You've got the number for our hotels in case there's an emergency?"

"I'm *fine.* Everything's under control." She licked her lips, wondering if this was the best time to broach one aspect of her resolution to get serious about life. "Ronnie?" she started, jumping in. "Are you still planning on, you know, cutting back?"

Ronnie sighed, then ran her fingers through her hair. "Yeah, unless I can find someone to take on as a partner. The problem is that bookstores make lousy investments. So potential business partners aren't exactly knocking down my door."

"So, what then?" Joan asked. "Three days a week?" Ronnie was finishing up her Ph.D. and looking into teaching. Plus, she wanted to spend more time with Jack. That, coupled with the store's lousy financial condition, had prompted her to consider cutting back the hours. A decision Joan didn't like at all.

"Something like that," Ronnie said. "I'll think about it after we get back. Don't worry, you know I won't cut your hours until you've found a job to make up the difference.''

Joan opened her mouth to press the issue, to tell Ronnie that she didn't want another job. That *she* wanted to be Ronnie's partner. Wanted a permanent stake in the business, and was willing to work her tail off to get it. But before she could speak, two honks from the taxi echoed through the store.

''I'm going to make us late,'' Ronnie said. ''Can it wait?''

''Sure,'' Joan said, trying for nonchalant. She'd just talk to Ronnie when she got back. And by then, Joan should be in a much better position to convince her boss that bringing Joan in as an owner made all the sense in the world.

''Great.'' Ronnie leaned over the counter and gave Joan a quick hug. ''I know you'll take perfect care of the place,'' she said.

Joan nodded, wished them a safe trip, and then found herself waving to an empty doorway.

They were gone. Now she was in charge.

It was a nice feeling, one she wanted to last beyond their four short weeks of vacation. She loved this store. Loved the musty smell of ancient books. Loved the customers who came inside, some with definite purpose, some who wandered aimlessly, drifting among the stacks until, as if by magic, they found a book that touched their soul. And she loved the variety of books that filled the shelves—literature, rare illustrated tomes, first editions of biographies and popular fiction, ancient travel guides and so much more.

And, of course, Joan loved the erotica. Ronnie's specialty was Victorian-era erotica, and she'd made a point of keeping the store well stocked with rare works from that period and others. During downtimes at the store, Joan would peruse the collection, reading everything from Anaïs Nin to D. H. Lawrence to *The Pillow Book.*

Joan had never considered herself uninformed where men were concerned, but this was new territory. The literature thrilled and inspired her, pushing her imagination to decadent limits. Unprofessional, maybe, but she couldn't help but get turned on by the graphic prose and the raw, unrestricted emotion generated within the pages. Forbidden fruit, and she loved studying it, learning about it, and, yes, losing herself in it.

Now Joan wandered among the stacks, the dim light from the single lamp at the front of the store causing provocative shadows to slide across the shelves in front of her as she moved toward her favorite section of the store—and her favorite book.

When she'd come to work for Ronnie fresh out of college, Joan hadn't been familiar with erotic literature. Oh, she knew it existed, sure. But she hadn't known it intimately. Hadn't known the value of a leather-bound edition, much less the depths of pleasure that the mere words on the page could impart. She shivered—a little tingle of anticipation—as her gaze scanned the shelves.

She found the volume she was looking for, a book from the late 1800s, bound in green boards and in pristine condition. *Very fine,* in bookstore terminology. The book's author was anonymous, but Joan didn't care. She was interested in the words, not who put them there.

And, oh, those words. Enticing and provocative, the stories could send her pulse racing as effectively as a lover's touch.

Licking her lips, she trailed her fingertip down the spine, delighting in the rough texture of the cloth, the slightly different feel of the title stamped in gold on the spine: *The Pleasures of a Young Woman.*

It was the kind of book she wished she could afford for herself, and yet she knew that would never happen. Extremely rare, the book was believed by scholars to be a collection created by some contemporaries of Oscar Wilde. The collection supposedly chronicled the erotic adventures of Mademoiselle X as she traveled from Paris to London. The young miss must have had quite an adventure, because the book read like a personal—very personal—anthology, describing in both words and pictures her forays into every erotic situation imaginable.

Such pleasures…

For just a moment, Joan wondered if her resolution

was foolish—if swearing off frivolous dating was simply a masochistic exercise that would do nothing more than keep her frustrated.

No.

With her eyes closed, she pressed the book to her chest. She wasn't swearing off men, just foolish dating of the wrong sort of man. Her door was wide open to Mr. Right. Absolutely. And if she met a guy with Mr. Right potential, they'd just have to take it slow and steady. That might leave her frustrated, but that was a state of being Joan could take care of on her own. And with a book like this…

Her fingers caressed the book as her mind wandered. It would be so easy. To take the book upstairs. To curl up naked under the crisp, cool sheets. And then to slowly, so slowly, open the book and drink in the pages.

She sighed, her body heating with anticipation. She knew this book. Every word, every nuance. Knew which passages were written with a light, almost humorous, hand, and which passages spoke to her soul, enticing her to stroke her breasts, her belly, and then dip her fingers down, down, down.

She shivered, and then, pulling herself together, firmly returned the book to its place on the shelf. It was almost dawn. She needed her rest. She did *not* need to lose herself in the steamy heat of erotic prose.

Still…

She paused, her hand hovering near the book. The

store *was* closed on Sunday, so she could rest all day if she wanted to. Besides, she wasn't sleepy. Just the opposite. She was wired. And the delicious prose was a distraction. Practically a necessity. After all, she'd sworn off casual sex and random dating. No little touches on the dance floor, no tickling of toes under the back booth at Xylo's. And absolutely no doing the wild thing. Definitely torture.

If she had the company of a warm book, though… well, a book and her imagination could make all the difference in the world.

Convinced, Joan slipped *The Pleasures of a Young Woman* back off the shelf. With a little sigh, she held it close, and then headed up the stairs to her apartment and to her bed.

A glass of wine, the faint strains of music and the pages of this book. *Heaven.* Or, at least, as close as she could get to heaven by herself.

"NOW THERE'S a looker," Leo said, pointing across the smoke-filled SoHo bar at a sultry redhead in too-tight Lycra who looked like she'd paid mightily for hair, tits and ass. "Bet she'd be a tiger between the sheets."

Bryce shot his attorney a frown, swirling the glass in his hand so that the ice rattled against the side. He took a sip, letting his gaze skim down the woman as the Scotch did a slow burn down his throat. "Not bad," he said, but without much enthusiasm.

"What's the matter?" Leo prompted. "Not your type?"

"I don't have a type," Bryce said. If a woman struck his fancy, he was more than willing to schedule time for her between the sheets. But a type? What was the point? Besides, he wasn't on the lookout for a woman to take up permanent residence in his life. He didn't have the time or the inclination, and he sure as hell didn't need the distraction.

"You ought to consider settling down," Leo said. "It would be good for your image."

"And she's the kind of woman I should install in a house in the suburbs?" Bryce asked, nodding toward the redhead.

Leo scowled. "No, she's the kind of woman you screw."

Bryce had to laugh. Leave it to Leo to get to the heart of the matter. Hell, that was what made him such a damn good attorney.

"Get it out of your system," Leo said, "and then come talk to me. Marjorie knows a lot of nice women who'd love to land you as a husband."

Bryce shook his head, interested in neither landing nor being landed. He didn't have the time for the sort of real relationship that would provide a solid foundation for marriage. Of course, considering his own parents' marriage, Bryce had wondered if that mythical solid foundation even existed. He'd thought they'd figured it out. And then ten years ago their idyllic life had crashed and burned. His mother had been having an affair. A long-standing one, apparently, and she'd run off with her lover. All along, she'd put up the perfect front, projected the perfect illusion. And Bryce had never even had a clue.

He didn't intend to let history repeat itself.

"What do you say?" Leo prodded. "The media's been all over this Carpenter Shipping deal. Three hundred jobs, Bryce. That's a lot of folks out of work. They're saying you don't care about the little people."

Bryce ran a hand through his hair. "I know what they say, Leo. I also know what they *don't* say—that whenever I buy a company and trim the fat, the business increases its efficiency by over twenty percent. That's a lot of extra cash in the investors' pockets, you know."

Leo raised a hand. "I know."

But Bryce wasn't to be placated. "And why doesn't the press ever report how we try to help the folks who end up out of work? No one ever does a story on how much severance we pay or about the people we've helped find jobs."

He knew he sounded defensive, but he couldn't help it. He'd worked his way up in the world, and no one had handed him any breaks. He'd bought his first building at nineteen, when he was just a kid earning a living doing construction. The ramshackle building in the warehouse district of Austin, Texas, had caught his eye—some hidden potential had been peeking out from under the grime and calling to him. He'd taken on extra jobs, pushing himself to the brink of exhaustion just so he could scrape together the down payment.

Two years later, he'd fixed the place up, sold it, and turned a tidy profit. He'd liked the cash, but, even more, he'd liked the thrill of putting the deal together. He'd reinvested his profits, turned a few more land deals, expanded into Dallas and Houston, and made his first million nine days shy of his twenty-fifth birthday. A small-town boy done good. And he'd just kept moving up from there.

Now Worthington Industries bought and sold companies. He had offices in Dallas, Los Angeles, Atlanta and New York, and spent more time traveling than he did in his own house. As president and CEO, Bryce would find a company with a good product and a solid core of staff, but one that was weighted down with debt and excessive overhead. He'd buy it cheap, clean it up, and then sell it again, often to the employee-investors, who ended up buying a company that was more streamlined and profitable than the one they'd started with.

Yes, some people lost jobs, but that was the nature of the beast. And business wasn't a charity. The point was to make as much money as possible for as many people as possible.

"I'm just saying that image is everything," Leo

said. "And your image would be a lot softer if you had a woman in the kitchen and a few kiddos playing in the backyard."

"I'm paying you to be my attorney, Leo," Bryce said, an edge to his voice, "not my public relations guru. And certainly not my social director."

"Marj has been on my case for years about finding you a nice girl," Leo said, ignoring Bryce's gibes.

"Who says I'm interested in nice?" Bryce retorted, mostly to egg Leo on. "Besides, my image is fine." At thirty-six, Bryce was one of the wealthiest and most eligible men in America. He had a love-hate relationship with the press, who—if they weren't busy reporting that his latest deal was a threat to the civilized world—tended to fawn all over him because of his looks and his money. Considering how many magazine covers his face had graced, anyone not in the know would think he was a movie star. He wasn't, although he'd dated a few on occasion.

"Investors like stability," Leo said. "Home and hearth and all that shit. Especially in an economy like this."

"Investors like profits," Bryce said. "Especially in an economy like this. And I give them that." He met Leo's eyes. "I'm not about to get married just so you can haul out some dog and pony show."

Leo held up his hands in surrender. "Hey, whatever. You're a big boy."

Bryce nodded and slammed back the last of his

drink. That he was. He glanced at his watch. 9:00 p.m. ''I want to go over the closing documents on the New Jersey property once more before tomorrow's meeting. Can you have them ready by two?''

Leo glanced at his own watch, then scowled. For a second, Bryce thought he was going to complain about getting home to his own wife and family. But then the attorney nodded. ''Not a problem. Hell, we can even work on the Carpenter deal. With the press breathing down our back and the employees threatening an injunction, I'm afraid it's going to blow up in our faces.''

Bryce frowned. ''It's your job to see that it doesn't.''

Leo just nodded. ''Don't I know it. Come on. Let's head back to the office right now. Jenny should be finished with the changes,'' Leo said, referring to his night secretary. ''We can proof the pages over a pot of coffee.''

Bryce shook his head. ''You proof them. That's what I pay you for. I'll be in at two to go over them with you.''

''What are you going to do between now and then?'' Leo asked.

Bryce flashed him a grin, then glanced toward the redhead. ''Work on my image, of course.''

THE ALARM ON Bryce's watch started beeping at one-forty-five, and the redhead shifted against him and pulled the pillow over her head, her bare butt grazing his hip. He slid out from between the sheets, careful not to wake her. After all, the woman—he'd forgotten her name—probably *was* exhausted. As Leo had predicted, she'd been a wild thing. Exactly what Bryce had needed to get his blood pumping for another twelve hours of posturing and chest thumping in the deep, dark jungle of mergers and acquisitions.

He found his boxers in a pile on the floor, her bra and panties wadded up with them. His trousers were hanging neatly over the back of a chair where he'd left them, the crease still perfect. He buttoned up his shirt, not bothering to tuck in the tail, and hung his tie around his neck before slipping on his jacket. Her apartment was at Fifty-fourth and Broadway, twelve blocks up from Leo's office. The September night was warm, and Bryce had energy to burn. He'd walk, then shower at Leo's office. If the papers were in decent shape, he might even have time to get a run in on the treadmill before the gladiators entered the ring for the nine o'clock meeting.

A single red rose was in a bud vase at the side of her bed. He'd purchased the flower for her as they were leaving the bar, and now he plucked it from the vase and laid it on the pillow beside her. Then he pressed a kiss to her cheek.

She really was a sweet girl, and he'd been grateful for the diversion, the few hours away from all things corporate. Now, though, it was time to get back to it.

The apartment was a studio, so he didn't have to go far to get to her front door. And as he stepped out onto the landing and pulled the door tight, he remembered her name. *Lydia.* Nice, but easy enough to walk away from.

For that matter, they all were. And as he started down the six flights of stairs to the street, Bryce silently cursed Leo. Because for the first time since his parents' divorce, Bryce was beginning to wonder if there really was a woman out there who could make him want to stay.

IT WAS THE HEAT that woke Joan up. That murky, almost liquid summer heat. The air conditioner must be on the fritz again. That sucked. Especially since the air conditioner wasn't even hers.

Other than the AC problem, Ronnie's place was nicer than anything Joan would ever be able to afford on her own. And it was only hers until Ronnie found a buyer for the fabulous flat—a one-bedroom apartment with a great kitchen and real hardwood floors.

Reluctant to leave—both the apartment and the bed—Joan moaned and stretched. *Pleasures* was still on the bed next to her, open to page one-twenty-three. She trailed her finger over the page, then closed her eyes, remembering the way the delicious, decadent words had played over her body, with a little help from her fingers, of course. She stretched like a cat, tempted to stay in bed and spend a few more wonderful hours with the book and her fantasies.

Naked, she twisted her body, trying to find a cool spot on the well-worn cotton percale. No luck. She sighed. Just as well. She'd already lazed away an entire Sunday, reading the book, watching television, sipping wine, and then reading some more. Now, it was the wee hours of Monday morning and time to get up.

With a little groan, she sat up, pushing damp curls out of her eyes before sliding off the bed and padding barefoot to the kitchen. She pulled the door open and stood there, letting the cool air dance over her skin. She shivered, a little chill racing up her spine as the thin film of sweat that covered her body started to disappear.

Her stomach rumbled, and she scoped out the inside of the refrigerator. Not much in there except Diet Coke and slightly limp carrots. She made a face, then grabbed a soda. At least it would fill her up and cool her off.

She closed the fridge and pressed the cool can to her forehead, closing her eyes and leaning against the stove. Who would have guessed she'd find heaven in an ice-cold aluminum can? Especially when she'd already found it in the hot, sultry prose of the nineteenth-century book.

Slowly, she trailed the can down over her nose, her

chin, down her neck to her cleavage. It felt wonderful, and she was just so damn hot.

Not that one twelve-ounce Diet Coke can was going to make much of a difference. No, if she really wanted to cool off, she might as well go downstairs to the bookstore and try to do some work. At least the bookstore had air-conditioning. And there was even food in the break room and an honest-to-goodness coffeepot.

Besides, she had tons of work to do. Ronnie had already been gone for almost twenty-four hours, which meant Joan had only twenty-nine days left to put her plan into effect. And if she went down now, she'd have four hours of uninterrupted work before she had to open the store.

She'd worked it all out in her head. She might have blown off college after only two semesters, but she had street smarts. The store hadn't been doing that great lately, so Joan's plan of attack was two-tiered. First, put together an exceptional catalog that would blow Ronnie away when she returned. And, second, increase the patronage—and the receipts—at the store.

The catalog was the easy part. The store did two catalogs a year, usually putting out a catalog focusing on erotica in the summer. Last summer, though, had been unusual, and the catalog had come out a few months late. Surprisingly, the issue had the best response ever, so Ronnie had decided to permanently bump the mailing date from August to early October.

Although Joan and Ronnie had worked together on it some, Ronnie had left most of the responsibility to Joan. And she intended to ace the project. Considering her rather intimate familiarity with the store's erotica inventory, she didn't foresee any problems on that score.

The business end was more troublesome. She made a mental list of her strengths and weaknesses. As her strengths, Joan counted her enthusiasm and the knowledge she'd gained about the industry over the past few years. Plus, she was a natural people person. Once a customer came into the store, she could usually get him or her to buy. Especially the hims.

Her weaknesses were worrisome. She didn't know much about running a business. Bookkeeping and strategizing and managing employees and all of that stuff, stuff that was so beyond her knowledge she didn't even know what questions to ask. She could learn, sure, but she had to learn *fast.* And she had to fit all of that learning in between doing the catalog and running the store.

She squeezed her eyes shut, fighting off the fear that she'd end up doing all this for nothing and Ronnie would either bring in another partner or knock the store's hours to so few that Joan wouldn't be able to afford to work there anymore. If that happened, Joan really didn't know how she'd stand it. She loved her job. All of it. The work fascinated and inspired her, something no other job ever had. And she adored Ronnie, who'd taken a chance on Joan when she was a twenty-year-old college dropout.

Over the years, Ronnie had been a great employer. But now Joan wanted more. She wanted to be a partner. And to do that, Joan needed to prove to Ronnie that she had the right stuff, that she knew how to run a business.

Considering she *didn't* know how to run a business, she wished she had a teacher, someone who could answer her basic questions and push her in the right direction. But she didn't.

But Joan had managed a lot of things on her own. She could manage this, too. It was simply a matter of finding the way.

2

JOAN SAT at the table in the break room, trying desperately to focus on the erotic books and ephemera spread out in front of her. Not an easy task. She'd contemplated and analyzed the stuff for almost three hours, and she'd made some serious progress on the catalog. Now, though, her concentration was fading. Instead of feeling clever, she was turned on.

She sighed, her fingers stroking a decadent illustration showing a woman touching herself intimately. A man—hidden in the shadows—gazed at the woman with lust in his eyes. The artist, who'd used a mixture of blacks and grays to draw out the shadows, was unknown, and Joan couldn't help but wonder if there really had been a model. Had she been spread out on the chaise, just so? Did she know the man was watching her? Did she fantasize that he would move slowly toward her and then press his hands on her breasts, her belly, trail fingertips down her until he cupped her sex, finding her wet and wanton, turned on by nothing more than the direction of her own thoughts?

Joan's body quivered, as if she could make the fantasy her own. The truth was, as much as she loved working in the store, the nature of its product could be quite, um, *distracting*. Then again, it was those very distractions that she liked so much.

With a little smile, she set the print aside before moving on to the remaining images scattered across the tabletop.

That one was definitely going into the catalog.

THE NEW JERSEY DEAL wasn't going to happen, not today anyway. Which meant that Bryce was stuck in Manhattan for at least another day, probably two. Maybe more.

He thought of his spacious house in Austin, built on five acres high in the hills overlooking Lake Travis. The manicured lawn, the swimming pool. And the trees. Lord, how he missed the breeze through the trees at night. He'd been in Manhattan now for a full week, and that was five days too long. He liked the city, loved its vibrant energy. But he loved his home more. And it irritated him that the delays keeping him in the Big Apple were all the result of sloppy work by his subordinates.

If this thing didn't get wrapped up soon, heads were going to roll.

With a frown, Bryce glanced at his watch. Not even 9:00 a.m. They'd called off the meeting thirty minutes ago, which meant that his all-nighter had been for nothing. Except for his brief sojourn in Lydia's apartment, he'd been up for thirty-six hours, doing little more than working on this deal, and now it was going to all fall apart because the company he wanted to buy was being fined by the EPA for dumping toxic waste. Not exactly the kind of acquisition the board of directors would approve of, and Bryce was livid that his people hadn't discovered the agency action sooner.

That was, after all, the whole point of due diligence.

Damn it all to hell. He ran a finger through his hair, cursing incompetence generally and wishing for the good old days when no one reported to him but himself. Back then, he knew the job had been done right because he was the one who'd done it. And on the rare occasions when there was a screwup, he knew perfectly well where to lay the blame. Right at his own two feet.

Now he had to deal with committees and boards and shareholders. He had a hell of a lot more money than he used to, but on days like this one, he had to wonder if he was having as much fun.

On the street to his left, traffic moved by at a snail's pace and horns blared, as taxis and commuters fought for space on the road. He'd been walking ever since seven, not watching where he was going. Just moving. The Big Apple wasn't really that big; he certainly hadn't feared he'd get lost.

And now here he was, somewhere far away from the familiar sights and sounds of Times Square or

Wall Street, pounding the pavement, working off his frustration on the streets of Manhattan. His shirt clung to him, damp from the combination of his exertion and the dense humidity. He still wore his suit jacket, and now he took it off, hooking it on a finger and tossing it over his shoulder. And as he did, he took a look around, delighted by what he saw—rows and rows of brownstones, the type that used to cover the island before the big conglomerates moved in with their skyscrapers and changed the skyline.

Bryce had no problem with skyscrapers. Hell, he owned three. But it was the older buildings that still held his heart. The kind of structures that not only reflected history, but *were* history. Homes and businesses that had stories to tell. The kind of stories that fascinated Bryce.

He slowed his pace, taking time to absorb the scenery and scope out the neighborhood. The family-owned brownstones had mostly been converted to apartments above retail space long ago. Even so, the area was quaint, and he began running through the familiar calculations—purchase price, the cost of necessary improvements, potential profit once he turned the property.

Not that deals were easy to come by in Manhattan. Prices were on the rise once again, and Bryce knew the market well enough to realize that finding a steal was unlikely.

Which was why the Apartment for Sale sign in the

bookstore's window surprised him. He paused, taking a step back so his gaze could take in the whole building. It was five stories of utter charm, with flower boxes under the windows on the fourth and fifth floors, and a wrought-iron railing leading up to the main entrance. The door was glass, and through it he could see a cozy antiquarian bookshop. The store's name, Archer's Rare Books & Manuscripts, was etched on the glass, and was also painted on a hanging sign that faced oncoming pedestrians.

He slipped his jacket back on, then stepped to the door and turned the knob. He pushed the door open, smiling to himself as the little bells tinkled to announce his entrance. Charming. He stifled a grin, anticipating the imminent arrival of a short, balding man with half-glasses and a ruddy complexion. Instead, he saw a tousled blond sex kitten in a tight black skirt, lavender glasses, matching fingernails and triple-pierced ears.

She stepped in from a back room, her huge blue eyes wide with surprise. "Oh," she said, a delightful blush blooming on her cheeks.

She drew in a breath and licked her bright red lips, and Bryce had the feeling he'd interrupted something, though he had no clue what. He half smiled. Maybe she kept a lover hidden in the back room. The thought amused him, and he couldn't help but wonder how those well-defined thighs and that perfect rear would feel under his touch.

"I—" She stopped, turning to glance at the entrance, her brow knitted in confusion. "Did you come in through the front door?"

"That's the traditional form of entrance, yes."

The flush on her cheeks deepened, and she shook her head, as if annoyed with herself. Her blond curls bounced, and Bryce found himself smiling.

"I'm sorry," she said. "Stupid question. It's just that the store doesn't actually open until ten. I stepped out earlier for a bagel. I must not have latched it behind me."

He turned and glanced again toward the door, for the first time noticing the Open/Closed sign that hung on a side window. Considering he could see Open, the sign facing the street must say Closed. "My mistake," he said. "I just barged in. I didn't even see your sign. You're right. You're not open yet."

She laughed, the delightful sound chipping away at the last vestiges of his bad mood. He wondered if he could think of something else to say that would amuse her, and then immediately wondered what the hell had gotten into him. Lack of sleep, most likely.

"I was beginning to think I'd lost track of time," she said. "I was…well, I was working in the break room." She glanced at her watch. "Wow. Already after nine o'clock. I didn't realize it was so late."

"That's early for most people."

She shrugged. "I have a lot to get done," she said, almost to herself.

Bryce could take a hint, though the thought of leaving didn't sit well. "I didn't mean to interrupt. I'll come back when you're open."

"Oh, no," she said, her voice breathy. "It's okay." She took a step toward him, her hand outstretched. She didn't touch him, but her proximity alone was enough to set the air between them humming. "You don't have to go." Her mouth drew into a frustrated line, and she pulled her hand back with a little shake of her head. "What I mean is, I've always got time for a customer." She stood up straighter and smoothed her skirt. "How can I help you, Mr....?"

"Worthington," he said. "Bryce Worthington."

She didn't react at all to his name, and Bryce said a silent thank-you. He wouldn't have been surprised to discover that Joan recognized either his face or his name. But she didn't and Bryce was happy to remain quietly anonymous. "And you are?"

"Joan Benetti."

"Benetti?"

She frowned. "Yeah. Why?"

"I was just expecting you to say your name was Archer." He nodded toward the sign. "This seems like a family-owned shop."

"Oh! Right, yes. Actually, it is a family name. My, uh, partner's father founded the store." Her brow furrowed. "Did you just come in to browse?"

He cleared his throat, wishing he *were* a customer. He had a feeling customer service would interest Joan

Benetti a hell of a lot more than real estate sales. "Actually," he confessed, "I'm not here to buy a book."

"Oh, really?" Her eyebrows lifted above the purple frames of her glasses, and a hint of a smile touched her lips. "Well, you don't look like you're selling anything..."

Bryce laughed. "No, I have a few questions about the building. Maybe I could ask them over breakfast?" He wasn't sure what prompted him to ask. All he knew was that the idea of spending more time with this woman appealed. "The coffee shop at the corner's open right now. And you have almost an hour before the store officially opens."

Her eyes danced behind her glasses, and she dragged her teeth over her lower lip, clearly hesitating. He leaned against one of the floor-to-ceiling bookshelves. "Well?" he pressed, hoping she'd say yes. The woman intrigued him and amused him. "What do you say? A breakfast date? If you're really in a crunch, you need to eat well. Vitamins, minerals." He let his gaze roam over the view she offered, taking in the bright red pumps—designer knockoffs, he was sure—and the shapely, stocking-clad legs. And considering how short she wore her skirt, there wasn't a lot left to the imagination. "Definitely a healthy breakfast," he said, forcing his eyes away before his gaze climbed any higher. "You need to be good to your body."

"Believe me," she said with a sultry grin. "I only put the best in this body."

"Exactly," Bryce said. He met her eyes, felt the tug of attraction zing all the way down to his groin. "You should come with me."

She glanced at his toes, then worked her gaze all the way up his body, her slow inspection almost as intimate as a caress. Clearly, she was sizing him up, and for the first time in years, Bryce actually wondered if he was up to her standards.

"No," she said quickly. "I'm sorry. I shouldn't have...I mean..." Another shake. "I'm sorry."

She might as well have kicked him in the gut. True, Bryce wasn't used to being turned down by women, but the hole left by her rejection was more than just a bruise to his ego. "Are you sure?" he asked. "Just breakfast. Innocent."

Once again, she tilted her head to the side. "No. I don't think so," she said, and Bryce wasn't sure if she was declining the date, or commenting that breakfast with him would be anything but innocent.

If she meant the latter, he had to applaud the woman's intuition. Because right then, Bryce's thoughts were a long way from innocent.

A long, long way.

STUPID, STUPID, STUPID!

Joan couldn't believe she'd almost blown her resolution so quickly and so thoroughly. She'd flirted with the gorgeous customer—sorry, *non*customer—as if there was no tomorrow. And she couldn't even console herself by saying that he had Mr. Right potential because she didn't know the first thing about him—other than that he made her palms damp and her stomach flutter more than any man she'd met before. But for all she knew, *that* reaction stemmed from the fact that, when he'd come in, she'd been up to her ears in erotic pictures and books.

Of course, even without that diversion, this was a man who made an impact. Bryce Worthington was positively yummy. Midnight-black hair and incredible violet eyes that seemed to see right through her. And he didn't just wear that suit. Instead, he seemed to have been born to it, filling it out in a way that made her mouth water. She'd always been a sucker for a man with a nice ass, and Bryce's rear end was pretty near perfect.

Joan's only saving grace was that she'd caught herself and had shut down her potential flirting frenzy before she'd really gotten going. Now she was all business, utterly professional. Just the way she intended to stay from now into the foreseeable future. Dull, maybe. But infinitely more practical.

She wiped her damp palms on her skirt. "How can I help you, Mr. Worthington?"

"Well, if breakfast is out of the question, I suppose I'll have to jump straight to the point. I came in be-

w the For Sale sign. Can you tell me about
rtment?''

Not really, I'm afraid. The building belongs to my partner. She's selling the two apartments and keeping the store.'' Mentally, she rolled her eyes. *Partner!* She wished. But that was neither here nor there where Bryce was concerned. It hardly mattered to this man if she was a partner or a clerk. The job was mostly attitude, anyway. And Joan had the attitude of an owner—and had been working her tail off like an owner, too. Now if she could just focus on books like *The Seven Habits of Highly Effective People* instead of tomes like Casanova's *The History of My Life,* maybe she'd actually manage to make the lie a reality.

Bryce's gaze was examining the store's interior, his inspection of the building as intense as his earlier visual caress of her body—a caress she still remembered with a little tingle.

''Do you think the owner would entertain an offer for the entire brownstone?''

She shook her head. ''Sorry.''

He nodded, but she could tell he was disappointed. ''I don't suppose you'd mind showing me around the flats anyway?''

She licked her lips, the idea of being alone with him in the apartment a little more than she could bear. Still, he did seem genuinely interested, and Ronnie would never forgive her if Joan shunned a potential buyer. "I need to finish up a project before the store opens. But you're welcome to go on up by yourself. The top apartment's unlocked and empty. I'm living in the fourth-floor flat, but feel free to wander through it." She handed him her key.

"You're sure?"

She shrugged. "Absolutely. No problem."

He caught her in that intense gaze once more, and she wondered if that was how deer felt, frozen in time but still caught up in something fast and furious. Because this was fast, and the beat of her heart was furious. She wanted him to go. To leave the room. He'd already almost made her break her resolution once. She didn't intend to let him succeed the next time.

After a second, he nodded, and she pointed him toward the interior stairs that led up to the flats. As soon as he disappeared from sight, she exhaled, releasing a breath she hadn't realized she'd been holding. His departure seemed to lift a weight, but, at the same time, it left her feeling oddly hollow.

No flirting, she reminded herself as she headed back to the break room. *Focus.*

And she did. She focused on her work for at least five solid minutes. Productive minutes, too.

But then she noticed the print again. The man watching the woman. The woman, looking so very enraptured. The man, whose face resembled Bryce's just a little.

Her body warmed, and Joan groaned, then shifted slightly on the chair to try to ease the pressure building between her thighs. She had one hell of a vivid imagination, but there were times when it seemed more like a curse, because right now she could imagine Bryce creeping down the stairs and moving quietly to the break room door.

He'd stand there, barely breathing, just watching. And as he watched, Joan would arch her back in her chair, her breasts thrusting forward as she grazed her fingertips lightly over her throat. The touch was a tease. Innocent, really, but promising so much more. Promising, that is, if he was good.

He was, of course. Very good. He watched. Just watched. And the watching turned her on. Made her wet. Made her sex throb in a way that demanded attention, demanded release.

Slowly, so slowly, she let her fingers wander down her body, caressing her breasts, following the smooth planes of her stomach down to her waist. The shirt was tucked in, and so she tugged it free, all the while wondering what he was thinking. Did he want to touch her? Or did he simply want the satisfaction of seeing her lose herself to pleasure?

With a little moan of anticipation, she slipped her fingers under the waistband of her skirt, then found the thin elastic band of her panties. She raised her hips, her body craving the touch. And as she licked her lips, her fingers pressed onward, over the coarse curls, finally finding her hot, wet core and—

Enough already! Her eyes flew open. He was in the building. Right above her. He could come back at any time. So what the devil was she doing?

Losing it. That's what she was doing. She was positively losing it.

Off to her left, she heard the scuffle of shoes, and then the distinct sound of a man clearing his throat.

Shit. In a microsecond, she was sitting upright, fear and embarrassment pounding in her chest. She turned to face the doorway. Sure enough, Bryce stood there, his eyes dark, an unreadable expression on his face.

Joan drew a shaky breath, wondering what she'd done. What he'd seen.

She glanced down, then exhaled in relief when she saw that her silk T was still tucked in. Thank goodness. It had all been in her head.

Please, oh please, let it have all been in her head!

"That was fast," she said, hoping her voice sounded normal. "What did you think?"

His mouth curled into an enigmatic smile. "It looked good."

Joan felt her cheeks warm, but she couldn't ask. Did he really mean the apartments? Or had he been watching her? The possibility was positively mortifying.

"This building's got great potential," he continued, and she relaxed a little. "I'm sorry the whole thing's not on the market."

"So you're not interested in just the apartments?"

"Probably not," Bryce admitted. "But I'll keep them in mind. Like I said, I liked what I saw."

He moved toward her then, and Joan swallowed, her entire body tightening as his proximity increased. After a second she saw his brow furrow and then his eyes widen with interest. He nodded toward the table. "Should I even ask?"

Joan glanced down. In her embarrassment, she'd forgotten about the erotica that littered the tabletop in addition to the one pen-and-ink print that she'd been holding. Now, she tried to imagine the scene through his eyes. The store had recently acquired a first edition of Casanova's *Memoirs,* which was a magnificent feat in and of itself. But on top of that, Ronnie had managed to locate eight of the original charcoal drawings used to illustrate an early edition of the famous book. Provocative images of men and women in the throes of passion. Copies of the drawings were scattered over the tabletop, along with lighter fare—naughty French postcards and colorful turn-of-the-century engravings showing women reclining in their wide skirts, with just a hint of what was going on underneath.

"A catalog," she said. "Our summer catalog always features erotica."

"Really?"

He was intrigued. She could see it in his eyes, and she couldn't help but shift into her sales mode. He was a customer now, some guy who'd come in to buy a first-edition Tony Hillerman and ended up buying Henry Miller and *Fanny Hill,* as well.

After a second, his gaze dipped to the table again, and he picked up one of the Casanova sketches, this one showing two women, both focusing every bit of their erotic attention on the man who lay between them on the bed.

"Interesting," he said, a wry grin playing at his lips.

Joan rolled her eyes. "*Men.* Funny how that card always seems to draw a man's attention."

"I'm not looking for two women," he said, meeting her eyes. "But I wouldn't mind spending some time with one good one."

It was a blatant come-on, and she pointedly ignored it, determined to stay all business. "Do you know much about erotica?" she asked.

"Well, I suppose that depends." The corner of his mouth twitched. "I have what I like to call hands-on knowledge of the subject. But formal book learning? Afraid not." His eyes met hers. "Maybe I'm due for an education," he said, his words flowing over her like warm honey.

She cleared her throat to keep the suggestive response that tripped to her tongue at bay. *The plan, remember? No flirting.* "I'm sorry the apartments aren't what you're looking for."

Disappointment flashed across his face. "Yeah," he said. "Too bad." After a moment, his expression shifted and he smiled, the simple gesture lighting his face. "Although I can't say it matters much. I might have stepped in to ask about the property, but once I was inside I found something much more interesting."

Joan's gaze immediately dipped to the tabletop. "It is fascinating, isn't it?"

He laughed, and she snapped her head back up, looking him in the eyes. "Not the drawings," he said, waving the sketch he still held. "*You.* You're my perk for the morning."

Her cheeks warmed. "A perk? I don't think I've ever been anyone's perk before."

"No? I'm surprised." He laid the sketch back on the table, then tapped it in the center with his index finger. "I'm serious, though," he said. "I bet there are a lot of things you could teach me." A sexy grin crossed his face. "For that matter, there are probably a few things I could teach you."

Joan didn't doubt that for a minute. This man made her tingle, and only a few weeks before she would have been a very eager student. Now, though, that kind of education wasn't on her agenda. Before she had the chance to tell him, though, the electronic tones of his cell phone trilled through the air. Bryce grimaced and pulled a tiny phone from his pocket. He checked the display, mouthed an apology, then answered the call. "Worthington."

Joan watched with interest. The man she'd been flirting with was confident, friendly and charming. The man on the phone was all those things and more. He had a presence about him, as if some invisible aura of command had dropped from the sky and surrounded him as soon as he'd answered the phone. Joan had no idea what he did for a living, but it involved a lot of money. Of that, she was certain.

"Dammit, Leo, I thought you had things under control," Bryce said. A pause, then, "No, I'm not thrilled. But if you really think this is the best route..." Another pause. "Well, I pay you to make these decisions, so just tell me what your recommendation is and stop beating around the bush.... Fine. I'm on my way."

He flipped the phone shut, shaking his head.

"Bad news?"

"I think so," Bryce said. "Because it means I have to go."

"Oh." She didn't know what else to say.

"Maybe I could buy you dinner?"

"Dinner?" she repeated stupidly.

He grinned. "You've heard of dinner, I assume? It's a ritual whereby people eat for nourishment, often finding entertainment in the company of others."

She made a face. "Yes, thank you. I've heard of dinner."

"Tonight?"

Her resolution flashed neon orange inside her head. She should say no, she knew that. But there wasn't anything resolution-breaking about dinner. Dinner could lead to Mr. Right.

Right?

Inwardly, she groaned. *That* was a justification if she'd ever heard one. And she fisted her hands against her own weakness, trying to bolster her resolve. This man was too sexy by half, and if she went with him to dinner, had a little wine, her resolutions would go up in a puff of white smoke. She'd be willing to bet on it.

"I'm sorry," she began, "but I've—"

"It's just that I find this so intriguing," he continued, nodding at the table. "And I'm a collector."

She frowned. "You are?" He hadn't struck her as the type.

"Well, not of erotica, but of first editions. You've started me thinking about expanding into new territories."

"Oh," Joan said, and then, when she realized just what a coup this man could be for the store's bankroll, *"Oh!"*

"Maybe you could pick out two or three of your best first editions. Something a serious collector needs. We could meet over dinner and talk about building my collection."

"Oh, yes. Right." Joan's head was spinning. Her guy resolution might be flashing neon orange in her head, but her profit resolution was lit up like a Broadway billboard, complete with soundtrack. If he was really thinking about buying three first editions...

She licked her lips, doing some quick math in her head. "Sure," she finally said. "Dinner sounds great. It'll have to be late, though. The store doesn't close until eight."

"So we'll eat at nine." He smiled, and Joan realized he was willing to accommodate whatever inconveniences she might throw his way. "In fact, why don't you bring three books and an invoice? I'm sure whatever you pick out will be perfect. I'll write a check at dinner."

"Oh." Joan stared, mildly flabbergasted. "Well, sure. Okay. I mean, I like a man who takes charge." It was a flirty comment, but she barely noticed. Right then, the possibility of an amazing sale overshadowed everything.

"Good. Then you should like me just fine." He slipped a card out of his breast pocket, then scribbled something on it. "I'm staying at the Monteleone," he said. "Do you know it?"

She nodded. Everyone in town knew the posh hotel on Fifth Avenue.

"There's a restaurant just off the lobby. It's fabulous. Talon. Does that sound good?"

"Um, sure." Really, it would be uncouth to leap

up and down for joy. Never in a million years would she be able to afford to eat there.

She took the card, the paper smooth between her fingers. On the back, he'd written *dinner, 9:00 p.m., Talon.* On the front, no job or company was listed. Simply a mobile phone number and *Bryce Worthington* as if that were all she needed to know. Hell, maybe it was.

"Then it's settled," he said. "A little wine, a little literature, a little erotica." He met her eyes. "Does that sound good?"

Joan swallowed. This wasn't a man people said no to. And, frankly, her entire body was screaming yes. Not that she intended to listen to her body. Bryce Worthington might be interested in a date—might be using the sale of erotica as a ploy to get her to dinner—but that didn't matter. Joan intended to stick to her guns.

She licked her lips. *Too bad for her.*

"Joan?" he pressed. "Are we on?"

She nodded. A silent, professional gesture. As if she delivered erotica every day of her life to men who made her nipples ache and her panties damp.

But her panties didn't matter. Because Joan was meeting this man *only* to sell him some erotica. And nothing else was going to happen.

Nothing at all.

A COLLECTOR*?* Bryce smiled, shaking his head as he slid into the taxi he'd hailed.

"Where to, buddy?"

He gave the driver the address for Leo's office, then settled back in the worn vinyl seat, thinking about his lie. The truth was, he owned one collectible first edition—Tom Clancy's *The Hunt For Red October*—that he'd inherited from his father, a submarine buff who'd bought one of the early copies before the book became a bestseller. Valuable, sure. But not exactly the sort of collection he'd suggested filled the nooks and crannies of his home.

Not that he felt any guilt about the fib. He'd seen the look on her face as she'd sat in the break room. A look of rapture, as if she was lost in thoughts just as erotic as the images scattered over the table. Her fingers hadn't moved from the gentle curve of her collarbone, but somehow Bryce had just known that in her fantasies, she was stroking and caressing her own soft skin. Touching places his fingers ached to touch.

In that moment, he'd been certain. He wanted to see this woman again, and he was thrilled that his earlier plans for the evening had been cancelled. He'd been invited by one of his model friends to attend the opening of a gallery, a high-profile fund-raiser. He'd been happy to do it. Going out with Suki was always relaxing. They'd been friends for years, but weren't the least bit attracted to each other despite the rampant rumors in the press.

Originally, he'd been disappointed when she'd called to tell him the benefit had been postponed.

Now, though, he was glad for the cancellation. It meant that his calendar was open. A rare thing, and extremely fortuitous, especially considering how much he wanted to spend the evening with Joan Benetti.

Unfortunately, she seemed less than enthusiastic about a date. Too bad. He'd sensed a chemistry between them that he didn't want to believe was one-sided. But she'd hesitated, and Bryce had turned to more creative methods to get her to go out with him. Well, what the hell? Best case, he'd have the woman in his arms. Worst case, he'd end up owning a few first editions. Either way, he certainly couldn't complain.

After all, the erotica on the table had been intriguing, to say the least. His body tightened merely from the memory, and he shook his head with wonder. Potent stuff.

Erotica had never been in his field of interest, but Bryce hadn't gotten where he was by turning away from new experiences. From what he could tell, Joan seemed to be an expert on the subject. And maybe, if fate was kind, Bryce could talk her into giving him a few lessons on the subject. He could hope, anyway.

And if the lessons were hands on, well, that would be all the better.

3

FIVE YEARS. He'd been without his beloved Emily for five long, lonely years.

A lump filled Clive's throat, just like it always did when he thought of her. His sweet Emily. So precious, so innocent.

She hadn't deserved to die.

Even now he could remember how she'd looked on their wedding day, her brown eyes so full of life, her near-black hair in stark contrast to the pure white of her dress.

His Emily. His love.

Slowly, Clive bent down and pulled the battered suitcase out from under the bed. He couldn't help but notice the carpet, worn and stained with God-only-knows-what. This was what he'd been reduced to, living in pathetic fleabag motel rooms that could be rented by the hour and had probably never even seen disinfectant. But it was necessary. The motels he'd chosen for the long drive from California to Jersey were cheap. That meant the clerks didn't even blink when you paid in cash, and they couldn't care less who was renting the room. That's what Clive wanted.

To be invisible. He'd need to be invisible if he was going to make this work.

Slowly, almost reverentially, he snapped the latches on the case and lifted the lid. He pulled out the flannel pajamas he'd used as lining and there, under the dark green material, he saw them—the shotgun and handgun he'd purchased specifically for this project.

He drew in a breath, anticipation mixing with nerves as the time drew near.

Soon, very soon, that son-of-a-bitch Bryce Worthington was going to pay.

"*BRYCE WORTHINGTON?* You're going out tonight with *the* Bryce Worthington?"

Joan squinted at Kathy as the younger girl brandished the pencil in her hand as if she was going to skewer Joan for not understanding the full impact of the date with Bryce. "Um, I guess so," Joan said. "I'm going out with *a* Bryce Worthington. Who is he?"

"You don't know?" Kathy shook her head in amazement. She was eighteen, a freshman majoring in English lit, and had recently been hired to work part-time in the store. Until today, she'd been in awe over the Dickens serials that Ronnie kept locked in the second-floor vault. Now, though, she'd transferred her enthusiasm to Joan's date. "You *really* don't know?"

Joan sighed. "I really don't know."

Kathy performed an exaggerated eye roll while exhaling, conveying the impression of being both disbelieving and put-upon. "He's like a bazillionaire. This self-made Texas businessman. And he's single. All those bachelor-type television shows have been trying to get him to go on, but he flat-out refused them."

Good for Bryce, Joan thought, her estimation rising a notch. She'd liked Bryce instantly and had had an instinctual feeling that he was a man with whom she'd get along great. Even after all of Kathy's oohing and aahing, she still wasn't sure she could place Bryce in the social hierarchy. The way Kathy talked, he fit somewhere between God and Ben Affleck. Big news, indeed.

"You've *really* never heard of him?" Kathy repeated, apparently unable to believe that Joan lived under a rock.

"Really," Joan said, more defiantly. She'd never paid a whole lot of attention to that rich celebrity stuff. She would happily follow the careers of musicians, actors and authors she liked. Even politicians, whether she liked them or not. But she did not follow the careers of big-shot businessmen.

Kathy just frowned, shaking her head a little.

"What?" Joan asked, sure the freshman was about to deliver a lecture about staying up on current events, though Joan was willing to debate whether Bryce's eligibility really was newsworthy. Especially since, as much as Joan might fantasize about a fabulously wealthy knight taking her away from all this, her odds of winning the Powerball lottery were significantly better than winning the heart of Bryce Worthington or any other man with a well-stuffed bank account. That was just too much like some unrealistic fairy tale.

"I just don't want to see you hurt," Kathy said. She wore no makeup, her fuchsia hair was pulled back into a sloppy ponytail, and she wore tight blue jeans with an equally tight tank top under a loose pink blouse. Even so, the impression she conveyed right now was matronly.

Joan ran her fingers through her hair, as annoyed as she would be if it were her mother giving her the third degree about a date. "There's no way I can get hurt, Kathy. It's not a date. I'm just meeting him to deliver some first editions. Purely business." That was her plan, and Joan didn't intend to veer from it.

"Uh-huh," Kathy said, clearly not convinced.

Joan rolled her eyes. "Oh, come on. We're just having dinner. Grown-ups are allowed to have dinner without having sex and dating and all that attached to it."

Kathy's eyes narrowed. "Where are you having dinner?"

"Talon," Joan announced, still reveling in what she considered a dining coup.

"Uh-huh," Kathy said, a mysterious edge to her voice.

Joan frowned. "What?"

"He's staying in the penthouse. He probably plans to ply you with wine and then take you up his private elevator for a quick tumble."

Joan certainly hoped not, because if that was his plan, she could already feel her resolve slipping away. "How do you know where he's staying?"

"Angela," she said, referring to her sister. For a second, Joan was confused. Then she remembered that Angela worked at the hotel. "He orders from the restaurant, and they send Angie up to deliver." She shook her head. "The penthouse is so huge she's never even seen him. She just leaves the tray in the living room. But she says it's worth it because he tips like you wouldn't believe."

"Well, then. See? He's nice."

Kathy snorted.

"Oh, come on, Kathy. What's the big deal? He wants to buy some books and learn more about the field."

"Oh, Joan-*ie*..." Kathy shook her head a little, then picked up a pile of books that had recently been entered into the inventory system. She headed for the stacks, but not before shooting Joan a look that practically screamed *you poor naive creature.*

Joan exhaled in frustration. At twenty-four, she always felt young in comparison to Ronnie, who'd already celebrated her thirtieth birthday. Around Kathy, though, Joan felt positively ancient. So she found Kathy's maternal tone a bit grating. "What?" Joan said, unable to prevent the note of exasperation lacing her voice.

"He's a total womanizer," Kathy said. "Last week he went out with some supermodel, and then the week before that it was some trust-fund type with all the right clothes and the right haircut."

"Oh." Joan ran her hand through her hair. "So what? The point of dinner is to talk about the books." All true. And yet she was having to convince herself even as she spoke. She didn't know the first thing about Bryce Worthington's background or habits, but she did know that something about the man blew her away. And the possibility that she was simply one in a long line of conquests rankled.

"Joan?"

She shoved the thought away, realizing she was being ridiculous. This wasn't a date. It was a business dinner. Business dinner, business dinner, business dinner. She said it over and over in her head, trying to make sure it stuck.

And that was when she realized...this dinner with Bryce Worthington wasn't just an opportunity to bring a little cash into the store, it was a boon to her overall business resolution. Not even twenty-four hours ago she'd been bemoaning her lack of business skills. If what Kathy said was true, this guy was even more on top of the business world than Joan had suspected.

And if Joan played her cards right, maybe she could get Bryce to give her a business lesson. She only hoped the price wasn't too high. Because as much as her libido might want to, she didn't intend to break one resolution in order to satisfy the other.

TONIGHT.

Clive held his hands out in front of him, the muscles in his chest and arms tight as he lowered himself slowly in a deep knee bend. Breathe in, breathe out. Calm. The trick was to stay calm.

He completed five sets of ten each, his balance never wavering. He was ready. He was calm. He was in control.

Slowly, he stood up straight, feeling remarkably light. "Tonight's the night, Em. Tonight, that bastard dies."

He closed his eyes and said a silent prayer. A prayer for success on his mission as he fought the evil that was Worthington. The man was vile. A pathetic, money-grubbing snake who didn't give a rat's ass about anything other than himself and his projects.

He was the reason Clive got laid off. And he was the reason his beautiful Emily had died. Oh, Worthington hadn't given her the cancer. But he'd killed her just the same. He took away her health insurance.

Took away their income. And in the end, his fragile, beautiful Em just hadn't had the stamina.

She'd left him. Left Clive all alone.

The papers had said that Worthington had made a fortune on that deal, and now there was talk of another takeover. Some shipping company. And Worthington was so smug. Business, he called it. Just business.

Bastard.

So he'd made a fortune, had he? Well, now it was time for Worthington to pay the price. And he was going to pay it to Clive. With his life.

Just like Em had paid.

BRYCE GLANCED at his watch, frowned, and lost his train of thought. Not hard considering the ridiculous array of questions the attorney had been throwing at him throughout this absurd, interminable deposition. He forced a smile. "I'm sorry," he said. "Could you repeat the question?"

"Certainly." The attorney on the other side of the table, a freckle-faced kid who reminded Bryce of Opie and couldn't be more than five minutes out of law school, turned to the court reporter. "Could you read back the question, please?"

As the reporter started to comply, Bryce held up his hand. "Wait." He turned to Leo. "Can we take a quick break?"

"Off the record?" Leo said to Opie, the words purportedly a question, but his tone allowing no room for dispute.

The young attorney nodded, waving his hand as if he was the king granting a pardon. Bryce pushed his chair back from the conference table, then headed out of the conference room, Leo at his heels.

"I need to go," Bryce said, cutting to the chase as soon as the door clicked shut behind them. "This has been dragging on for hours now. It's a bunch of BS, and I've got better things to do with my time."

Leo ran a hand through his hair, looking decidedly uncomfortable. Bryce knew the reason, of course. The shareholders in Carpenter Shipping had hired themselves a big-shot attorney and had gotten a temporary restraining order that morning. In an effort to resolve the dispute and keep the deal moving, Leo had offered to present Bryce for a deposition.

Bryce had agreed. But his patience had worn thin. "He's not even focusing on the sale," Bryce said. "The kid's fishing, and he's wasting time doing it."

Leo nodded. "I know. The kid's green. But so far he hasn't established one element of his claim. There's nothing to support converting the restraining order into a permanent injunction, but if you walk out now, he'll just tell the judge he wasn't able to finish." Leo shrugged. "I'm betting another hour. At most."

Bryce frowned. As much as it rankled, he knew Leo was right. "Fine," he said. "But I'm supposed to be on a date. Give me a few minutes to make a call." As soon as Leo headed back into the deposition, Bryce turned on his cell phone and dialed the restaurant. The maître d' promised to relay the message to Joan—he'd been detained and would call her in the morning.

He hated doing it, but he didn't want her sitting there waiting. Opie might have only an hour's worth of questions, but he might have three. And although it was late, Leo wanted to keep going rather than spend the day tomorrow in depositions—time that should be spent on the New Jersey project.

He switched off his phone and headed back into the abyss. He hoped Joan was available tomorrow. Because if Opie was making Bryce miss out on dinner with the woman altogether, then the young attorney was really going to see the full force of Bryce's wrath.

THE HOSTESS HAD SEATED HER even though Bryce wasn't there yet, but now Joan was wishing she'd waited in the bar. She felt horribly conspicuous sitting all alone at the small, intimate table. Just feeling that way bothered her. She'd been everywhere—from truck stops to black-tie affairs—and this was the first time she'd felt truly out of place.

Hoping to ignore the feeling, she glanced into her tote at the books she'd chosen. She'd brought several so that he'd have a choice. Most were standard fare—early editions of works by Lawrence and Miller and others. The basic building blocks of a serious erotica collection. The third, though…well, the third was *Pleasures.* Her favorite book.

If she'd been feeling contemplative, she would have wondered about her motivations in bringing a book that both fascinated and turned her on. Fortunately, she wasn't feeling contemplative.

She took another sip of her wine, then nibbled on a bread stick to counteract the alcohol that was fast going to her head. She was on her second glass. A mistake, probably, but she hated just to sit there. And so when the waiter had offered the wine, she'd simply accepted.

For the umpteenth time, she glanced at her watch. Nine-twenty. Damn.

She pulled out her cell phone and checked the display screen, wondering if perhaps she'd missed a call. She hadn't, of course, and then she remembered that she hadn't given him her number. She had his, though. She hesitated to use it, the act of actually calling to ask where he was too wounding to her pride.

But she supposed she'd rather suffer a slight bruising to her ego than sit there all night sipping wine and getting wasted. She punched in the number, and the phone rang and rang, finally switching to voice mail.

She clicked off, not bothering to leave a message. What would she say? *Where are you?* That was too pathetic. *Have you stood me up?* That was too angry.

Nothing quite fit, and so she said nothing, intending to wait five minutes and simply try again.

After four minutes, the maître d' approached. "Ms. Benetti?"

Joan licked her lips. "Yes."

"Mr. Worthington regrets that he has been unavoidably detained and will be unable to meet with you this evening."

"I see." Joan forced the words out, Kathy's warning about Bryce ringing in her ears.

"Would you care to order? Mr. Worthington made it clear that you were to have anything you requested. His treat, of course."

"Of course," she repeated, her mouth dry. She shook her head. "No, thank you. I'll just finish my wine and get going." She smiled at the waiter, the picture of a woman used to these pesky scheduling issues. As soon as the maître d' backed off, Joan opened her purse and pulled out a few bills. As she got up, she tossed them on the table. And then, with as much pride as she could muster, Joan walked out of the incredibly fancy, horrifically lonely restaurant.

"WHY ARE YOU still here?" Joan aimed the question at Kathy. She'd left Kathy with the master key to the store, letting her close up the shop on her own for the first time. She'd never anticipated that Kathy would still be there at 10:00 p.m., sitting in the leather armchair, a book open on her lap.

Kathy shrugged, looking more than a little sheepish. "My roommate had a scarf hanging on the door, and I didn't feel like going to a bar."

Joan nodded in understanding. Obviously Kathy's roommate and her boyfriend wanted some quality time.

Kathy cocked her head, then closed the book on her lap. "Actually," she said, "that's a lie."

Joan blinked. "What is?"

"The scarf. I could go home. But I wanted to wait for you."

Joan turned, noting for the first time that the door to the stairwell leading up to her apartment was open; Kathy would be able to see her whether she came in through the store or the back entrance. "O-kay," she said slowly. "What's up?"

Kathy sighed, then used the arms of the chair to push herself up. She headed to the counter, walking slowly, like someone condemned. "I got my roots done last week, and I started reading this article on Botox while I was waiting." She grabbed a magazine off the counter as Joan wondered what this had to do with anything.

"And?"

"And I didn't finish the article, so I kept the magazine—Leona doesn't care—and I finished it today. Then I was flipping through, and...well, *look.*" She shoved the magazine at Joan. It was folded over to one of the interior pages.

Joan looked, and as she did, her mouth went dry. "That son of a bitch," she whispered.

"I'm sorry," Kathy said. "As soon as I read the article, I figured you'd be back early. I wanted to wait for you."

Joan grimaced. The article—more a series of photographs, really—showed Bryce with a runway model, apparently known in the fashion world as Suki. According to the text, Bryce and Suki had plans to attend the gala opening of some new SoHo gallery. An opening that just happened to be tonight.

Bastard.

So much for her thin hope that he'd simply gotten held up somewhere. Or been trapped in an elevator. Or gotten rushed to the hospital for food poisoning.

"I knew he was a womanizer," Kathy said. "But I never thought he was a two-timing womanizer." She grimaced. "I'm so sorry."

Joan ran her fingers through her hair, certain that the curls she'd forced into place were now going wild. Well, too bad. "Who gives a flip?" she asked. "He's a prick. I don't want to have a date with a prick."

Kathy raised an eyebrow. "I thought it wasn't a date."

Joan grimaced, irritated with herself for thinking of Bryce in datelike terms. "Date or not, it was still a waste of my time."

Kathy grimaced. "He is a prick. And a jerk, too, if he thinks he can get away with this." She glanced down at Joan's tote. "And he was just leading you on with the bit about buying some books? Now *that* was truly tacky."

That it was, Joan thought. And he shouldn't get away with it. "I've got half a mind to march down to that gallery and make him buy these books," she said. She'd let the floodgates of her anger open, and now her face was heating with rage. She paced the room, arms waving as she got caught up in her cause. "How dare he waste my time like that! Who the hell does he think he is anyway?"

Kathy nodded vigorously, murmuring both encouragement and condolences. "You should," she said. "But you'd never get near him. Not at the opening. It's invitation only."

Joan frowned. Kathy had a point. "So what should I do? Blow it off? Hang out in the alley behind the gallery? Leave obscene messages on his voice mail?"

For a moment, Kathy's face remained blank, then a slow smile spread across her face. "How about throwing him completely off guard? Be waiting in his living room when he comes back from his little fling with Suki."

Joan laughed. "Oh, yeah. That would be great." She could just see it. Her reclining on the hotel's plush sofa, the erotic anthology open in front of her. He'd step inside the door, his supermodel on his arm. And then she'd look up and say, "Why Bryce, darling, did you forget we had a little business to attend to?''

She shook her head, dissipating the image. ''Too bad.''

''What?'' Kathy asked.

''Too bad I can't really do that.'' It was a lovely fantasy, one that was perfectly safe, too, since there was no way she could get into the billionaire's hotel room.

''Why can't you?''

Joan lifted an eyebrow. ''Duh. The man's staying at the Monteleone. In the penthouse.''

''Yeah,'' said Kathy, her tone suggesting that Joan was an idiot. ''And Angie works there, remember?'' She grinned. ''So what do you say? Want to go pay a visit to Bryce Billionaire?''

Joan licked her lips. It was a stupid, reckless, silly plan. And she went for it in a second.

''Absolutely,'' she said. ''Let's go find Angie.''

4

BY THE TIME Bryce made it back to his hotel room, complete exhaustion had set in. He'd just spent eight solid hours answering inane questions from an over-eager pup of an attorney, and even though it required no physical energy whatsoever, mentally the whole process had been taxing. He was drained and all he wanted to do was take a shower, drink some wine, kick back with the *Wall Street Journal,* and then fall asleep.

Only the thought of Joan kick-started his energy level, and he toyed with the idea of trying to track her down. Unfortunately, he didn't have her phone number.

As he passed through the suite's ostentatiously decorated living area, he pulled off his tie, then tossed it on the settee. He pulled his cell phone out and dialed information, looking for the number of Archer's Rare Books & Manuscripts. The operator connected him, and the store's machine picked up, dutifully reciting the location and hours of operation. But no human came on the line, and there was no way to leave a message.

Damn.

Frowning, Bryce clicked off. And that's when he noticed that he'd missed a call. It had come in at about nine-fifteen. Which meant that it could have been Joan, calling to ask where the hell he was. A little surge of anticipation shot up his spine as he punched the button to display the caller's information.

Nothing. Just *Mobile Caller* and a number in the 212 area code. Well, at least he knew the caller was in New York. That narrowed the field to about a million possible persons. He was only interested in one.

Since there was no other way to know, he dialed the number. One ring, two, three, and then, "Hi, Joan here. Well, not really. But just leave a message and I'll get back to you." A pause, and then she added, "If you're lucky," in a voice that evoked images of black lace and satin sheets.

Bryce grinned. He barely knew the woman, but already he knew the message was just her style. Once the beep sounded, he spoke. "Joan, it's Bryce. I'm sorry about tonight." He gave her a quick rundown of why he'd been detained before continuing with, "Can I make it up to you? Give me a call." He left his number again, as well as the number at the hotel, then clicked off. If he didn't hear from her by noon, he'd send a dozen roses to the store. He hadn't met a woman yet who could resist roses.

He glanced at his watch. Eleven-thirty. Good. Just enough time for him to take a shower. By the time he got out, the waitress would have delivered his wine and Brie, and he could relax. If he was lucky, maybe Joan would return his call. If that were the case, he'd happily exchange a relaxing night in bed for...well, a not-so-relaxing night in bed.

Until then, though, he was going to take it easy. He headed for the bedroom and tuned the television in the armoire to the financial news, half listening as he stripped down. He found a pair of sweats and a package of T-shirts in the bottom drawer of the dresser. He tossed the clothes onto the bed, then headed into the bathroom.

With Joan on his mind, Bryce stepped into the shower stall, succumbing to one universal truth—if there wasn't a woman around to relieve a man's tension, the next best thing was a scalding hot shower.

"YOU GUYS ARE going to get me fired," Angie Tate said. "I'm supposed to already be off my shift." She shook her head, one fist propped on her hip as she aimed a sharp stare at Joan and Kathy. If it weren't for the tug at the corner of her mouth and the gleam in her eye, Joan would have guessed that Angie would nix the project right then.

But she didn't. Instead, she just pointed at Kathy. "You, go on home. And you," she said, switching her aim to Joan, "if anyone even looks like they might have a clue what we're up to, then you're my best friend from California, you're in town for the week, and I thought you'd get a thrill riding up to the penthouse with me."

Joan nodded, still unable to believe her good luck.

"So you'll really do it?" Kathy asked.

Angie shrugged. "Sure. I mean, it's *Bryce Worthington.* If I can't have him, it might as well be someone I sort of know."

Joan shook her head. "I don't want him. I just want to give him a piece of my mind."

"Uh-huh," Angie said, but she didn't look like she believed it. Her gaze drifted from Joan's stiletto heels, up her stocking-clad legs, and then over the extremely short, extremely flirty dress that Kathy had helped her pick out. "Purple," Angie said, as if that summed everything up.

Joan supposed maybe it did. Purple was seductive and passionate. Joan wouldn't have let herself cross over into date-land with Bryce, but he didn't know that. And she wasn't above letting him know exactly what he'd missed out on. "Purple," she confirmed.

Angie grinned, the expression knowing, and Joan smiled back. Then she frowned and turned toward the elevator. "So I'm just going to ride up with you?" The plan seemed way too simple.

"Sure. There're always lots of people hanging out in the hall. You can wait here while I get his tray, and then we'll go up together." She shrugged. "I'll let you in the room. What you do once you're in there is your business," she added with a leer.

"What I'm going to *do* is chew the bastard out," Joan said. "If he's even there." She turned to Kathy. "He's probably still at the opening."

Kathy shrugged. "So you wait."

"I've never seen him," Angie explained. "I mean, not in person. But he's got a standing order for wine and cheese at midnight. I leave it in the living room, and he gets it after I've left."

Joan licked her lips. "He'll know you let me in. Who else could have? What if he gets you fired?"

Angie tugged at the collar of her uniform. "Believe me," she said. "It wouldn't be the end of the world."

Joan frowned, but didn't back out of the plan. The truth was, she wanted this too badly. And not just the chance to read Bryce the riot act. No, even though she wasn't about to admit it to either Angie or Kathy, she simply wanted to see Bryce one more time. He might have acted like the biggest jerk in the world, but he was a jerk who'd made one hell of an impression on her.

"Okay," Kathy said. "Give me a hug for good luck, and I'll hit the road."

Kathy gave her a squeeze, and then Angie looked her up and down. "You ready?"

Joan glanced from one to the other. "Ready," she said. "Let's get this show on the road."

ANGIE WAS RIGHT. The employee-only hallway between Talon and the service elevator was anything but employee only. Lots of folks seemed to be coming and going, and twice Joan had to press herself flat against the wall to avoid being knocked down by a room-service waiter racing down the hall with a cantankerous cart. Twice she saw the hotel manager—Angie had pointed him out—and both times Joan tried to conjure the appearance of someone busily standing around in a hallway. She must have succeeded, because the manager paid no attention to her whatsoever. Good.

Actually, everyone essentially ignored her, too busy going about their various tasks. Which was more than fine with Joan. Except for the occasional appreciative glance toward her cleavage, she was pretty much invisible to the waiters careening down the hall with their carts and the uniformed hotel staff passing through on their way to do hotel-type stuff. A guy in a baseball cap pulled low over his eyes, and toting a duffel bag, parked himself near the elevator, but he didn't look at her, either. Just kept staring down at his ugly combat boots.

Joan shifted her weight from one foot to the other, antsy. This was stupid. She'd never been a vindictive person—well, okay, maybe a little—but was it really worth it? So he'd stood her up. So he was a jerk. Big freakin' deal. She'd dated tons of jerks, but she never staked out their apartments.

All true, but this was business. And the business world was dog-eat-dog.

Mentally, she rolled her eyes. She might not admit it to Kathy, but she had to admit it to herself. And the painful truth was that she probably would have walked away—would have backed off from pure bitch mode, gone home, and drowned her sorrows in a bottle of merlot—if it weren't for the memory of the piercing heat of his eyes, and the way her stomach had done somersaults when he'd looked at her. *Before* he'd stood her up.

Her head had wanted the meeting for business purposes…but a secret little part of herself had wanted so much more.

Anger and indignation made her stay. That, and the fact that Angie suddenly slammed backwards through Talon's kitchen door, a tray of wine and cheese balanced on her hands. "Okay, Joan. You ready?" Angie glanced at Joan as she shifted the tray to one hand, then pushed the elevator's call button.

Joan sucked in a breath and replied with the only possible answer. "Abso-freakin'-lutely."

IT WASN'T SUPPOSED to happen this way. *He* was supposed to get on the elevator with the waitress. Every night he'd watched, and every night she'd gone up to Worthington's room alone.

But not tonight. Tonight she'd gotten on the elevator with some little bitch—and before Clive could react, the elevator doors had slammed in his face.

Damn it all to hell.

Now what did he do? He didn't know. He'd had it all planned out, and she'd gone and screwed it all up for him.

Deep breaths. That's what he needed. He told himself to take long, deep, calming breaths. Yes. Right. Okay. It would be okay. The solution was obvious, so obvious that he almost laughed out loud.

He'd simply come back tomorrow.

Worthington ordered the same wine, the same cheese, every single night. The girl would deliver it tomorrow, just like she had today. And the blonde wouldn't be there. The little waitress would be all alone, and she'd do exactly what he told her. He'd make her let him into Bryce Worthington's hotel room…and then he'd be face-to-face with the man.

And then—

"Can I help you?"

Clive started, but remembered to keep his head down. "I'm…I'm just—"

He shifted, and the damn duffel tumbled free, the butt end of the shotgun spilling out.

"Okay, buddy, hands on your head." The guard was all bluster and action now, and Clive knew that he'd totally messed up.

He lifted his left hand up slowly. But his right was still in his jacket, his hand tight around the butt of his Glock, his finger hard against the trigger. He fired. And the guard went down.

Screams filled the hall, and Clive knew what he

had to do. In one swift move, he yanked the baseball cap off and pulled down the stocking that he'd worn as a skullcap under the hat. The nylon pressed tight, crushing his features. He clutched the gun, then waved it in an arc to encompass the crowd.

To his right, the elevator dinged, and the door slid open. Clive whipped around, pointing the gun at the occupant. "You," he said, then picked two others from the hallway. "And you, and you. And don't anyone do anything foolish—I've got the place surrounded with gunmen," he lied.

With the barrel of the gun he gestured them toward the door to the kitchen. "Go."

They went.

Clive swallowed, bolstering his courage. He had to do this. The blond bitch had ruined everything, and now Clive had no choice at all. Not if he wanted to get out of this alive.

"YOU'RE ON YOUR OWN."

Angie's final words still echoed in Joan's ears. They'd arranged *The Pleasures of a Young Woman* on the tray with the Brie, the wine and the single crystal wineglass, and then Angie had slid it onto the coffee table. The whole setup made something of a statement, actually, and Joan had to laugh at how completely behind her Kathy and Angela had gotten, how indignant they were on her behalf. But their support didn't change anything in the end. Joan was going through this alone, trapped in a living room that looked like something Louis XIV had spit up.

She took a deep breath and maneuvered the room, skirting the settee and chairs formed into a conversational grouping around the solid, dark wood coffee table where Angie had slid the tray. As Joan looked down at it, the full scope and idiocy of her plan caught up with her, and her knees went weak. She collapsed into one of the richly appointed armchairs, her heart pounding so hard she was certain Bryce could hear it even from inside the shower and over the low drone of the television.

She swallowed. What in heaven's name had she been thinking?

From the other room, she could hear the delicate clatter of water in the shower stall. He was in there—maybe alone, maybe not—naked and steamy, while Joan was out in the living room acting like some mindless junior high schoolgirl. Dumb. This had been a very dumb plan.

She needed to get out of there. Escape with her dignity intact and swear Kathy and Angie to secrecy. Maybe she'd see Bryce again, and maybe she wouldn't. But if she did, she wanted assurances that no one would ever tell him that Joan Benetti had broken into his hotel room bearing erotica.

She stood up, fully intending to grab the book and head toward the door. But as she got to her feet, she realized the water had stopped. Not only had the water stopped, but the antique-gold louvered doors to the bedroom were starting to open. He was coming into the living room!

With no time to get to the door, Joan hit the floor and crawled behind the couch. She scooted backwards until she was between the outside wall and a folding screen with a scene of some royal dude at court. If she got out of this mess, she was going to have a long heart to heart with the hotel's decorator. The room was positively gaudy.

She sat on her heels, able to see only a sliver of the room through the gap where two panels of the triptych were hinged together. The bedroom doors creaked, and Joan held her breath. And then he walked into her field of vision. Bryce Worthington, wearing nothing more than a towel around his waist.

Joan swallowed, trying very hard not to make a sound when her initial reaction was to mew like a kitten. Jerk-wad or not, the man was yummy. From her hiding place, Joan could see every delectable inch of him. He'd toweled off, but not completely, and his body glistened in the soft light, the tiny droplets of water making him gleam like some Greek god.

His coal-black hair seemed even darker now that it was wet. With his hair slicked back, his face had lost the slight softness that his natural waves had brought. Now he looked ruthless. Predatory. And undeniably sexy. A tingle eased up Joan's spine and she bit the side of her thumb as Bryce moved through the living room. His stride was confident, controlled, and she couldn't help but wonder what those powerful hands would feel like on her body.

His skin was a deep bronze, in sharp contrast to the white hotel towel wrapped around his waist, and she imagined him spending hours in the sun, lounging next to a bikini-clad supermodel. A smattering of hair covered what appeared to be a rock-hard chest, tapering down to a thin line that eased below the fold of the towel like an arrow pointing the way toward home. Her fingers itched to touch him, and she wondered how many women had followed that path down to the prize hidden under the terry cloth.

The towel ended abruptly midthigh, and his legs were just as hard as the rest of his body. Bryce was no flabby businessman spending all his time behind a desk. He worked out. And Joan could picture him on a racquetball court, a thin sheen of sweat glistening over his body, as he pulverized the competition. Bryce had the air of a man who got what he wanted, both on and off the job.

Joan frowned, allowing herself one quick moment of self-pity. Apparently *she* wasn't something that Bryce had wanted.

She shook her head, banishing such ridiculous thoughts. Joan had never been a woman who moped around wondering if guys found her attractive. They did. She knew that, and there really wasn't much point in playing the naïve little cookie. But that didn't mean that every guy would want her. And if Bryce didn't want her, then it wasn't going to dent her ego.

No, what pissed Joan off was the arrogant, casual way he'd tossed her aside...and the carrot he'd dangled in the form of a possible sale. *That,* my friend, was rude.

Joan swallowed, only then remembering the book. They'd set it on the tray, right under the plate of Brie. And Bryce was heading for the coffee table right then.

The wine was uncorked, and he poured himself a glass, took a sip, then started to reach for the knife to cut a slice of cheese. She knew the instant he saw the book. He frowned, a curious expression crossing his face as he reached down to lift the plate. The book came into view, and his head popped back up, his eyes scanning the room before settling on the door. Another frown. Clearly, he assumed Angie had delivered the book, then left. But he had to know that Joan was behind it.

Was he looking for her? Was he regretting breaking their date?

With pronounced casualness, Bryce set the book on the edge of the coffee table, then cut some Brie and put it on a cracker. He took a bite, then sat in the chair that faced the triptych. Joan tensed, afraid he could see her through the gap, but he wasn't even looking her direction. Instead, he was looking at the book. He picked it up carefully, then leaned back in the chair, the leather spine cradled in one hand.

Both his feet were on the floor, his knees slightly apart, and from Joan's crouched position she had a direct view to the shadowed space between his legs. She licked her lips, unable to tear her eyes away. She'd fallen under some erotic spell, and she shook her head, disgusted with herself for wanting a little peep, while at the same time she silently prayed for him to shift just enough so that she could see beyond the murky gray of shadows.

It would be so apropos, really. Her favorite passage in the book was the one where Mademoiselle X, upon visiting friends in the country, finds herself wandering alone down a garden path. She gets lost—of course—and ends up by a small stream. There's a stone bench, and the gardener is there, resting in the shade in the late afternoon sun. The air is heavy with the scent of lavender, and the young miss crouches behind a dense bush, barely hidden from the virile workman.

She wants only to watch him—to let her eyes feast on this fabulous specimen of masculinity, one off-limits to a person of her elevated class. Soon, though, she experiences so much more than she could have imagined. The gardener, overheated from his work, is lying along the bench. His eyes are closed, but a smile plays along his lips. The young miss has no idea what he is thinking, but she imagines that he is thinking of her. That he has seen her in the gardens and taken a fancy.

Soon, the gardener lifts a hand, wiping his brow.

His shirt is unbuttoned, and has fallen open, exposing his chest and stomach, both a deep brown, undercut with a hint of red from long hours in the sun. His hand, weathered and calloused, rests on his stomach, just above the waistband of his pants. She watches as he breathes deep, his chest rising, as his nimble fingers loosen the laces that hold up his breeches. He slips his hand under the cloth, his fingers stroking his shaft as his eyes close in an expression of tentative ecstasy.

As the young miss watches, the man's sex stiffens, jutting free of the thin work pants. His ministrations quicken, his breathing becoming more rapid. The man turns his head, his eyes opening, his lids heavy with passion. He faces her, staring straight at her hiding place, a seductive grin playing across his lips. And then, with an inviting smile, he speaks two words: "My lady…"

The memory of the passage teased Joan, and she shook her head, drawing her own thoughts back to the present. She was being ridiculous. From what she'd seen in the store, quite a bit of erotica focused on women touching themselves as men looked on, both hidden and not. Few pieces dealt with women watching men. *That* was why she was thinking of this passage. Because it was academically unusual. That was all. Not because she harbored any fantasies that Bryce would notice her. And certainly not because she harbored fantasies that he would pull her skirt up, toss her across the couch and have his way with her.

Really.

With determination, she forced her eyes away from the forbidden zone, as if that would force her mind off thoughts of his hands stroking and teasing her. Instead, she looked at his face. Even when he thought he was alone, his expression remained guarded, but she could see the glimmer of interest in his eyes, the slight bobbing in his throat as he swallowed. He was intrigued. No doubt about it. And she fought a spurt of frustration laced with anger. If he hadn't been such an arrogant son-of-a-bitch, standing her up the way he had, they might have been able to have some serious fun exploring the nuances of erotica. From a purely academic standpoint, of course.

He flipped a few more pages, then tossed back the rest of his wine. He used a napkin to mark the page, then returned the book to the coffee table. The towel was too small, even for his narrow hips, and it was pulled tight across his lap. Joan might not be able to see under the towel, but considering the telltale white tent now formed by the cloth, Joan could safely surmise that Bryce Worthington was at least a tad turned on. Well, good. She hoped he had to take a freezing cold shower. That would serve him right.

As if that was exactly what he planned to do, he stood up, then turned and headed toward the double doors leading to the bedroom. After a second, she heard the television click off and silence filled the room. She shifted slightly to the left and was able to keep him in view. The doors were pushed open, and now she had a clear view of the bed, except for one side of it that was partially blocked by the settee. She considered standing up behind the triptych to get a better view, but dismissed the idea immediately. Too risky. And what was it she wanted to see, anyway?

That question was answered almost immediately. With one quick tug, Bryce pulled the towel off and tossed it on the floor. He stood there naked, his back to her, and Joan stifled a gasp. In all of her dating history, Joan didn't think she'd ever seen a butt quite that perfect. Nice and tight and totally sexy. Just as she'd suspected, this butt ranked a perfect ten.

But then Bryce turned, and that's when Joan *really* saw perfection, and coherent thought vanished from her head like dandelion fluff in the wind. Like Michelangelo's David, Bryce's entire body was hard and perfect. Her own body tightened as pure liquid heat rushed through her veins, pooling between her thighs with a dull, persistent throbbing.

She couldn't take her eyes off him. Her fingers longed to touch him. To stroke, to caress. And, most of all, to be touched by him in kind.

Not a welcome reaction. Not under the circumstances, anyway.

She was here for payback, not to get turned on. She needed to get out of the room, to run, to escape back to her life where her head worked like a normal person's instead of like an addle-brained simp's.

In the bedroom, Bryce stepped into a pair of gray sweatpants which he tied at the waist. When he completed the outfit with a crisp, white T-shirt, Joan released a silent sigh of relief. He was still sexy as hell, but at least the clothing added one more barrier between him and her overactive imagination.

She hoped he would head into the bathroom so that she could make a run for it. But no. Instead he headed back to the living area, looking far too much like a man who was ready to settle in for the night with a good book and a glass of wine.

Joan shifted, her legs already slightly numb from her crouch. This was not good. If he decided to drink a few glasses of wine and read the book, she could be stuck there all night. Her entire body ached at the thought, and she imagined each limb falling asleep in turn until she was curled up behind the triptych, unable to move, and finally found in a petrified state by the maid when she came to clean. Not a pretty picture.

The only reasonable solution was to show herself, to come out from behind the screen and confess to everything. And suffer the consequences, the most obvious of which would be major embarrassment. Not high on Joan's list, but unless Bryce stood up and headed back into the bedroom, that looked like the only viable option.

That was when Bryce poured himself another glass

of wine...and Joan knew that she was stuck. Time to face the firing squad.

Her cramped thigh muscles weren't at all excited about cooperating, and she was slow to stand up. Right as she was rising, the clear tones of Bryce's cell phone rang out through the room. The man sighed, then pushed himself off the sofa. Unable to believe her good fortune, Joan watched through the gap as he moved into the bedroom and disappeared. A second later, she heard his voice.

"Worthington."

No more footsteps. No nothing. Apparently Bryce was having this conversation in the bedroom.

Go.

Joan didn't argue with herself. She forced her cramped legs into gear and hightailed it for the door, thankful for the plush carpet that muffled her pounding feet. When she reached the tile foyer, she slowed, tiptoeing the rest of the way to the door. She gripped the doorknob, turning it slowly until the latch gave, then yanked the door open, preparing to race down the hall toward the staircase.

She didn't get far. Her path was blocked by two uniformed men in flak jackets carrying automatic weapons, their badges held aloft. She took a step backwards, her heart pounding in terror. Her immediate thought was that she was being arrested for breaking and entering. "I'm—"

"Hostage situation, ma'am," the taller one said. "We're going to have to ask you to stay put."

5

THIS COULDN'T BE happening. There was no way that this could possibly be happening.

Joan stood there, her mouth hanging open. She managed only one word. "But—"

"I'm sorry, ma'am," the tall one said. He really did sound sorry. The short one just stood there, his gun at the ready. Joan tried hard not to look at it.

"We're going to have to ask that you stay in the room, keep your door and windows locked, and don't step out onto the balcony." He spoke loudly, and Joan twisted to look back over her shoulder, wondering if Bryce had heard them. But there was no sign of him, and she could hear the faint timbre of his voice drifting in from the other room.

Thank goodness for small favors.

Joan swallowed, tiny pieces of her composure finally coming together to form a coherent whole. "No," she said, shaking her head for emphasis. "No, you don't understand." She kept her voice at a whisper. "I have to get out of here. I'm not even supposed to be here in the first place."

Neither man seemed particularly sympathetic to her

plight. They just apologized again and started to step back from the door.

"No," Joan said, cringing at the frantic tone in her voice. She reached out to brush the short one's sleeve. "Couldn't you move me to another room?"

Wariness flashed across the guard's face, and he paused, staring at her with intense eyes. "Is there a problem, ma'am?" he asked, his tone low and serious. "Are you in danger?"

Joan realized the direction his thoughts had turned and cursed her stupidity. "No, no," she said. "Nothing like that." God, what a twit. Some maniac had taken people hostage and she was worried about embarrassing herself in front of Bryce. "It's fine," she said. "I'm fine."

"*We're* fine." Bryce's voice. She felt the pressure of his hand against her shoulder. Well, hell. "What's going on?"

BRYCE WAS TRYING HARD to remain calm, but it wasn't easy. There were armed police in his doorway and a woman he desperately wanted to touch looking like she just as desperately wanted to escape.

"A gunman has taken a number of hostages on the ground floor," the officer said, and Bryce felt his stomach roil.

He tightened his fist. "Do you know the gunman's goal? Money? What does he want?" His pulse picked up tempo. Had the gunman come for him? He'd never been the target of any sort of crime before, but he couldn't discount the possibility now, not with the Carpenter deal being so hot.

"No sir, we don't."

"I see."

The officer must have seen concern reflected on Bryce's face, because he continued. "We've secured the remainder of the building and sealed off the gunman's location. Standard operating procedure. At the moment, we have no concerns for your safety, but you'll need to stay put."

Bryce licked his lips, his gaze darting to the back of Joan's head. She still hadn't turned to face him.

"And you should be aware that we may find it necessary to cut phone service or power to this grid."

"Where? I mean, what's his location?"

"The kitchen," the short cop said.

Joan turned to look at him then, a pained look on her face. In one fluid movement, he reached out, realizing her knees were giving out on her. "Hey, whoa there." He caught her around the waist and pulled her close, liking the way she felt in his arms.

As soon as he was certain Joan was steady, he turned back to the officers. "Thank you," he said. "We'll be fine."

The officers nodded, then Bryce shut the door. He looked deep in Joan's eyes and saw fear reflected back at him. A fear he wanted to quell.

"Are you okay?" he said.

Her brow furrowed. ''Don't you want to know why I'm here?''

He had a feeling he knew. He'd stood her up, and she'd come to tell him off. ''Later. Right now I want to make sure you're okay.'' He stroked the tip of his finger along her jawline. ''Are you?''

''No,'' she said, and he had to admire her honesty.

''Oh, babe.'' He pulled her close again, and wrapped his arms around her. She resisted at first, but then she relaxed, taking the comfort he offered. He liked the feeling, too. Liked knowing that he was helping, even if just a little. That was a power of its own, and somehow more potent than every bit of authority he wielded in a boardroom or around a negotiating table.

He stroked her hair, breathing in the clean, soapy scent. ''You heard the officer, right? We're safe up here.''

She nodded, then pressed her palms to his chest as she pushed back and looked him in the eyes. ''I know. But *hostages,* Bryce. What if Angie's been taken hostage?''

''Angie?'' The name was familiar, but he couldn't place it. And then he remembered—the girl who delivered his cheese and wine. She knew Joan. And suddenly he knew without even asking how Joan got into the penthouse.

Angie, however, hadn't stayed with Joan. And that

meant that she was down there somewhere in the hotel. Possibly in the kitchen.

The possibility didn't sit well at all.

Determined to make sure Joan felt safe, he reached out, then pushed a wild lock of hair off her forehead. "Angie's fine," he said.

Joan smiled, a tremulous gesture. "How can you be so sure?"

He allowed himself one grin. "It's just my nature."

At that, she actually laughed, and the noise lifted his spirits more than he would have thought possible.

"I can see that about you," she said. "I bet you say something is going to turn out one way and it just does."

"Absolutely," he said. "So you can trust me on this."

She ran her fingers through her curls. "I wish I could believe you...."

"Come on." He took her hand and urged her forward, steering her into the living room and urging her down into the plush armchair he'd been sitting in only minutes before.

He could feel her eyes on his as he went to the phone and picked up the handset. No dial tone. Damn. With a sigh of frustration, he grabbed his cell phone from the counter and dialed. The phone rang, and then Gordon's voice answered, but the man himself wasn't there. "Gordon, it's Bryce. Give me a call on my cell when you have a moment. It's about this hostage situation at the Monteleone. Thanks."

He clicked off, then looked at Joan with a tiny frustrated sigh. "No luck. Sorry."

"Who did you call?"

"Gordon Graves," he said. "He reports directly to the chief of police. He's a good friend, and I'm sure he'll help, but I can't get through to him right now." He tried a smile, but didn't quite succeed. "I'm sorry."

"Thanks," she said. "I appreciate you trying at all." For a brief moment, she looked disappointed. And then her eyes widened. "*The police.* Of course! I have a friend who's a cop." She reached out her hand. "Pass me your phone."

TYLER DONOVAN GROANED and pulled the pillow from off his face. Rolling to the side, he groped for his cell phone, then pounded buttons indiscriminately until he hit the one that stopped that damned infernal ringing. "Donovan," he mumbled.

"Did I wake you?"

Donovan ran his free hand through his hair, his brow furrowed. The voice was female and familiar, but he couldn't place it. "Huh?" Not brilliant, but it would have to do.

"It's Joan," she said.

Donovan was awake now, everything clicking into place. "What's up, kid? You okay? Something happen with Jack or Ronnie?'' His partner had married Joan's boss, and over the last year, he'd gotten to know the kid pretty well.

''I'm at the Monteleone,'' she said. The way she spoke made him think that should mean something to him.

''The hotel?''

''Do you know what's happened? Can you tell me anything?''

Donovan was on his feet now, his mind humming. ''Sorry, kid. I don't know a damn thing.''

''Hostages,'' she said, and he reached immediately for the television remote control.

The situation was all over the news, and Donovan's stomach twisted. ''Shit, Joanie.''

''I'm stuck in the penthouse, and I think—'' Her voice broke. ''Oh, God, I think he may have a friend of mine.''

Donovan hit the mute button for the TV. ''What's your friend's name?'' She told him, and he scribbled it down. ''I'll call you back.''

''No. No, please. Can I just wait?''

He shrugged. ''Sure. No problem.'' He put the cell phone down then headed to his land line. Two minutes later, his stomach was in knots. ''Joan?'' he asked, coming back on the line. ''He's got somewhere in the neighborhood of five to ten hostages. He shot a guard, but the man is stable and expected to recover. We think our gunman's working with snipers outside the building, but we don't have confirmation. And for all we know, there may actually be two or three guys in there, not just him."

"Angie?" Joan asked, her voice weak.

"That's the good news. Your friend had already clocked out by the time the perp made his move. They don't have any reason to think she's in there."

Joan's sigh of relief was audible. "Thanks, Donovan. I owe you."

"Are you okay?"

"I think so," she said.

"You'll be fine, kid. Just don't worry." Platitudes, but what the hell else could he say? He didn't even have a clue as to what the full situation was.

"Thanks, Donovan. You're the best. Go back to sleep."

She clicked off, and he eyed his couch. Tempting. He was still exhausted, and he wasn't on the hostage team. But, no. Instead he grabbed his keys and headed to the door. He might not be on the team, but he damn sure intended to find out what was going on.

"SHE'S NOT THERE." Joan smiled, her relief so obvious that Bryce's heart just about melted.

"I'm glad," he said.

The phone rang, and they both looked at it.

"I thought it wasn't working," Joan said.

"It wasn't." He moved toward her and answered the phone. She didn't move away, and her proximity fired his senses, making him want to reach out. To touch her. Instead, though, he answered the phone. "Worthington."

It was a sergeant with the hostage rescue team, and Bryce listened as the officer ran down the situation in more detail than the two uniforms at the door had done. He nodded, said, "Thank you," then hung up and turned to Joan.

"They've shut down phone service to the building."

She raised an eyebrow. "They *called* to tell us that?"

"Service with a smile," he said.

"Why?"

He shook his head. "I didn't ask. Presumably, they want to make sure no one in here leaks information to the media. And that the gunman can't talk to anyone but them."

"What about cell phones?" she asked. "Couldn't someone talk to the media on their cell?"

Bryce just shrugged. Personally, he had no desire to talk to the media about this or anything else. Inevitably they would connect the situation with his presence in the hotel. He knew what the questions would be: Did his high-profile takeover of Carpenter Shipping somehow spark the gunman's actions? Was the gunman seeking retribution? Was he some former employee injured in a takeover? Anything to find a headline. And, once again, Bryce would have to explain how he worked his tail off trying to make businesses run better, and in situations where folks did get laid off, he did his damnedest to make sure they found other jobs and kept their benefits for as long as possible. The whole situation was out of control and he fought the urge to lash out, worried about the hostages and hating the madman who'd put them there.

"Bryce?" She squinted up at him. "The media?"

He flashed a smile. "Sorry. Woolgathering. I really don't know what the police are thinking."

She made a face. "I feel so awful for those hostages. And, well, I'm scared."

At her words, he felt an overpowering need to keep her safe. To make sure she felt protected and secure in the circle of his arms.

He nuzzled her hair. "Everything will be fine," he said. "We're a long way away from the kitchen, and the officer said that the building has been evacuated."

At that, her eyes went wide. "They've got a strange definition of evacuate since we're still in here."

He grinned. The woman didn't miss a trick. "The penthouse is on a different elevator. Apparently they think there's a risk in evacuating us, but that we're perfectly safe staying right here."

"A risk?"

"They didn't explain," he said. Though he could guess. If he was the target, they'd want him up high with guards at every entrance point, and far away from what was happening below. "Right now, though, we're safe. We are, however, stuck." He headed to the coffee table, then poured a glass of wine, holding it out to her as an offering. She looked at him warily, then took it.

He poured a glass for himself, sipped it, and then watched as she took a gulp of the wine, then another. Then one more after that. When the glass was empty, she stared down at the crystal before finally lifting her gaze. She wasn't quite able to meet his eyes, however. Her cheeks colored pink, creating a striking contrast against her pale skin and golden-blond hair.

She took a deep breath. "We're really stuck, huh?"

"It looks that way. The priority is the hostages, not inconveniencing us."

She nodded. "Of course."

He frowned. "This will be all over the media. I need to make a few calls, let people know I'm okay. How about you?" he asked. "Do you need to use my cell phone?"

She shook her head. "No one knows I'm here except Kathy, and I don't remember her number. But she's Angie's sister, so she'll know to ask the cops." She ran her teeth over her lower lip. "If we're still stuck in the morning, I'll call my parents. But I'm not going to worry them at midnight."

He nodded, then picked up the phone to call Leo. No answer. He left a quick message that he was fine, and clicked off. There were others he could call, but Leo could handle damage control in the morning.

As he deposited the phone back on the counter, Joan glanced over her shoulder toward the door. "So how long do you think we'll be here?"

Bryce shook his head. "I don't know." He suspected a long time. Over the years, he'd become friends with a great many cops, and he was familiar with the procedures. Unless they suspected a bomb, they were going to keep everyone in place while they assessed the situation. Their goal was to solve the problem without loss of life. If it took an hour, great. If it took four days, well, so be it.

Bryce's body tightened at the thought of four days alone with Joan. He wanted her, no doubt about that. At the store, he'd been attracted to both her looks and her sass. He'd wanted to touch her, to make her laugh. And now, knowing her fear, he wanted all that and more. He wanted to take her someplace where she wouldn't be afraid. But since they couldn't leave, the only place to take her was right here. To stroke and kiss and caress her until she forgot everything but being in his arms.

Joan, though, might have other plans. She'd spurned the idea of an actual date with him, despite his efforts to entice. He had no idea why she'd held back—the idea that she simply wasn't attracted to him was too depressing to even consider—and he didn't know if she'd changed her mind. He hoped so. Lord, how he hoped so.

The color in her cheeks deepened. "I guess I owe

you an explanation,'' she said. ''I mean, it looks like we may be stuck together for a while.''

''Stuck,'' he said. ''You make it sound like torture.''

She rolled a shoulder. ''Maybe you'll end up thinking it is. I mean, I did break in.'' She took a deep breath. ''The truth is, I was pissed off,'' she added, as cool anger flickered in her eyes.

He frowned. ''I can see being annoyed that I broke our date, but why would you be angry? These things happen.''

Her eyes widened. ''These things happen?'' she repeated, her voice rising. ''Come on, Bryce. Even if you couldn't be honest with me this afternoon, at least be honest now. I mean, we're stuck here together. It'll be a lot more bearable without the lies.'' She crossed her arms and waited.

She'd completely lost him. He had no idea what she expected him to say. ''I'd love to help you out here, but you're going to have to give me a clue.''

She tossed her head back in exasperation, then stared at him intently over the purple rims of her glasses. ''A clue,'' she repeated. ''You want a clue. Okay. Fine. How's *Manhattan Today* for a clue? The opening of the Quentin Barker Gallery. Supermodel. Any of that ring a bell?''

Bryce fought a smile. ''As a matter of fact, it rings a lot of bells.'' He dropped down into a chair, propping his right foot on his left knee as he leaned back against the cushion and looked at her.

"And..." she prompted, her hand making a little twirling motion as she urged him along.

"And Suki's a very nice lady."

She shook her head. "Fine. If you don't want to tell me, that's fine. I suppose it isn't any of my business anyway except that you said you were going to buy first editions from me. You dangled this huge carrot and then you went and scheduled the date with me on a night when you already had a date with her. So, yeah. I was pissed."

He nodded. "I can see why you would be."

Her eyes narrowed. "Really?"

"Absolutely. And I think there are a few things I need to clear up. First, I got the distinct impression from you that we were having a business dinner, not a date. Not my preference, I admit, but I was willing to accommodate." She opened her mouth, but he held up a finger and went on. "Second, I did not have a date with Suki. I had one, but it was cancelled about two weeks ago."

She squinted. "Really?"

"Absolutely. The opening's been postponed a week. I begged off since I don't intend to stay in Manhattan that long. I believe George Clooney will be Suki's new escort."

"Oh." Joan licked her lips, and he could practically see the wheels turning in her head. "And she doesn't mind?"

"Not in the least."

"Oh," she said again. She sank down into the plush sofa cushions, then slipped off her shoes and tucked her feet under her. She didn't say anything, but kept her eyes on him as she grabbed a silk throw pillow and hugged it to her chest. After a moment, her brow furrowed. "So when you asked me to dinner, you didn't already have plans?"

"None at all," he said. He nodded toward the Louis XIV desk on the far side of the room. "Nothing except to sit at that desk, read over some documents, and have a glass of wine. If I was feeling wild and crazy, who knows? I might even have had two glasses."

"Shit," she whispered.

"No, it's okay," he said with a grin. "I'm used to my rather dull existence."

That drew a smile. "Yeah, I bet you are."

"You can't believe everything you read in the press," he said.

A wry grin touched her lips. "I'm learning that one the hard way." This time she did meet his eyes, and though he could sense genuine embarrassment, he also saw an undercurrent of strength. "Like I said, I'm sorry. But if there was no opening, then why—"

"Did I dump you?"

"Well, yeah. I mean, if you wanted to break a

da—'' She licked her lips. ''A business dinner with me, then why—''

''I can't imagine any man actually wanting to break a date with you,'' he said, cutting her off.

''Really?'' Her mouth quirked into a lopsided grin. ''You're only saying that because I've behaved like a total spazz and you're trying to make me feel better.''

''Sweetheart,'' he said, ''I'm not that much of a gentleman.'' That actually drew a laugh, and he gave himself a couple of points on his imaginary scoreboard. ''Besides,'' he added, ''I have proof.''

''Proof?''

''Checked your cell phone recently?''

Her brow creased. ''Well, no, actually. Not since I left the restaurant. And I turned it off once Kathy and I set out to find Angie.''

''Do you have it? Check it now.''

She got up and went back into the foyer to rummage in the totebag she'd dropped there. After a second, she emerged with a phone, and she carried it and the bag back toward the table. She pressed a button, then turned away from him with the phone pressed to her ear. When she turned back, her expression was contrite.

''That was a really sweet message,'' she said. ''Depositions, huh?''

''Sadly, yes.''

''I'm really sorry I didn't get your message,'' she

said. ''I would have much preferred coming over here by invitation rather than...um...''

''By stealth?'' he offered.

''That's one way of putting it,'' Joan admitted.

Bryce hid a smile. He'd seen the sparks that could light up those deep blue eyes. He could just imagine the fire that smoldered just below Joan's surface, ready to burst forth when she got angry or excited...or, for that matter, turned on. Now *that,* Bryce thought, was a fire he'd like to stoke.

''We can still do it that way, you know,'' he said.

''That way?''

''Sure.'' He nodded to the door. ''You can come over, we can have a glass of wine, sit down to look at the books and discuss my soon-to-be erotica collection. We can't do dinner, I'm afraid, but we can have a lovely evening, just like we'd originally planned.''

''We'll forget all about the past few hours, then?''

''They won't even be a dim memory,'' he said.

''Well,'' she said. Her lips pressed together and then she nodded. ''To be honest, I think I like that plan a lot.''

''Great,'' he said. He nodded toward the foyer. ''Let's go.''

She frowned, but followed him.

''So here we are,'' he said. ''I've just answered the door and let you in.''

An odd expression crossed Joan's face, somewhere

between amusement and confusion. "All right," she said, standing in the foyer looking absolutely beautiful. "Um, so now what?"

Bryce stared at her, something tickling his memory. And then it clicked. He cocked his head, regarding her. "What did you mean earlier," he asked, "when you said that you'd changed your mind and were trying to leave?"

"Oh. I..." She trailed off into a shrug. "Nothing."

"Nothing," he repeated. "I don't think so."

She didn't respond, just licked her lips and stared at the tile floor.

With purpose, he moved back to the living area, then plucked the book off the coffee table. *"The Pleasures of a Young Woman,"* he said. "One you picked out for my collection?"

"It's quite rare," she said, still in the foyer. "It would be quite a coup for a collector."

"I'll keep that in mind," he said, never taking his eyes off hers. "But the book was here when I stepped in from the shower. And if you came in with the book..." He trailed off, his eyes scouring the room for possible hiding places. There were no closets. The kitchenette, perhaps? Behind the counter?

Her gaze drifted to the three-paneled screen, and he knew. "That is the perfect spot," he said. "Unless of course I'd decided to walk over here to turn on this lamp." He demonstrated, heading toward the lamp right then, and ending up on the rear side of the screen.

"But you didn't," she said.

"No," he agreed, "I didn't." But the words were a mere murmur because, at that point, he wasn't thinking about what *he'd* been doing, but about what *she'd* been up to. From the front, the gaps in the panel were barely noticeable, cleverly disguised by the artist as elements of the triptych. From this side, however…

He bent closer, pressing his eye to the gap. The view was quite clear. Both of the chair he'd been sitting in and the broad expanse of the bedroom.

When he came back around the screen, he saw that she was nibbling on her lower lip. He fought a smile. No use showing his hand. "Your hiding place?"

"Yes."

"Quite a view," he said.

Again, she simply answered, "Yes." This time, however, the words were accompanied by a deep blush.

He moved back to the chair, sitting down and facing her. He ran his hand over his chin. He needed a shave. She watched, not saying a word, though she walked slowly—cautiously—toward him.

"I, um, wasn't really expecting…I mean, I didn't come up here to see…I mean—"

He leaned back. "Did you like what you saw?"

She drew in a deep breath. Whether expressing relief or drawing courage, he wasn't sure. ''Hell yes,'' she said after a bit.

Bryce wanted to laugh, but he forced himself to keep a straight face. ''Glad to hear it,'' he said. ''But now you've seen me naked, and I haven't had the same pleasure. That hardly seems fair.''

She cocked her head, wary, but didn't say a word.

''Don't worry about it, though,'' Bryce said. ''I've figured out a solution.''

''You have?'' she said, the wariness shifting from her eyes to her voice.

''Of course,'' he said. He let his gaze roam over her, starting at her stocking feet and trailing all the way up to eyes that were watching him with just a hint of trepidation. ''I think, sweetheart, that you're simply going to have to take off that dress. Get naked, Joan,'' he said. ''After all, fair is fair.''

6

NAKED.

Joan swallowed. *Naked* meant blowing all her plans and promises. *Naked* meant sultry gazes and tender caresses and finding absolute pleasure in the arms of this man. This man, whose intense gaze had grabbed her from the first moment they'd met. This man, whom she wanted desperately even though it meant breaking her own resolution.

She would have liked to blame it on the circumstances, but that was only part of it. She'd wanted him from the first moment she'd seen him, when the air between them had seemed alive with electricity. She'd had willpower then. Now, though…

Now her willpower had been swept aside. All she knew was that her resolution didn't matter anymore. She didn't even remember why she'd made it. Something about Mr. Right. But that could be Bryce, couldn't it? He was smart, articulate, rich. A real American prince. An honest-to-goodness exception to her stupid little resolution.

In the back of her mind, she knew that was idiotic. What would a guy like Bryce want with a woman like her over the long term? Still, she could dream. *Wanted* to dream. Because in dreaming she didn't have to think about what was happening in reality. And right then, she didn't want to think at all.

"Well?" he prompted. "Come on. Show a little skin." He crossed his arms in front of him, his expression completely serious except for the slight twinkle in his eye.

It was that twinkle that was her undoing, and she grinned. This was a man with whom she would enjoy flirting. And so much more, too.

She met his eyes. "Skin, huh?"

"Skin," he repeated. This time the smile in his eyes reached his mouth. "Let me know if you need help with buttons or hooks or clasps."

"Got experience in that regard, do you?"

"A tad, yes."

She licked her lips. "Naked," she said, meeting his eyes. "As in *naked* naked."

He nodded. "I think it's only fair."

She conjured a sultry grin. "Never let it be said that I'm unreasonable." Slowly, she lifted one foot onto the soft cushion of the sofa. She flexed her muscle, pleased with the nice definition in her calf. She'd spent four nights a week in the gym before the summer had hit in full force, wanting to be ready for swimsuit weather. It had been hell, but considering the heated way Bryce was now looking at her, she decided it had been worth it.

First, she slipped off her shoes. Then with slow, deliberate movements, she slid her skirt up, finally revealing the clips of the garter belt that held her stocking in place. She pressed her thumb against the pressure point, opening the clip. With her palms, she slid the stocking down her calf, wondering if she should be humming a striptease tune.

As soon as she reached her ankle, she arched her foot, slipping the silk garment all the way off. She straightened up, her foot still on the sofa, and faced Bryce, the stocking dangling triumphantly from her forefinger.

"Voilà," she said, keeping her voice low and breathy. "Skin."

"Nice," he said. His gaze traced up her leg, leaving a streak of palpable heat in its wake. "But I was looking for a little bit more."

"Hey," she said, adding a note of indignation to her tone. "I had to work for my eyeful." She nodded toward the screen. "Do you have any idea how hard it is to sit still in a crouch behind that thing?"

He glanced toward the screen, then smiled a slow grin. "So we're negotiating?"

"Why not? You're a businessman. You want to see skin. I want..." She trailed off with a shrug.

"What?" he asked. He moved toward her, and suddenly his hand was cupping her calf. She inhaled, a sharp intake of breath that probably didn't serve her well if she was trying to act calm and collected.

But the truth was, she was feeling anything but calm and cool. Instead, she was feeling hot. And antsy. And the press of Bryce's palm against her skin only made this vague, sensual longing all the more intense.

While one hand stayed on her leg, the other cupped her waist. He leaned in, his breath tickling her ear, and she caught the faint scent of wine. "What do you want?"

Joan swallowed. She could barely think, couldn't answer. All she wanted was this man's touch. The situation enticed her, and memories of her favorite erotic passages drifted through her head. Bryce was the unknown Victorian Englishman who wrote *My Secret Life.* He was touching her, devoting long and intimate attention to every part of her body. Every secret erogenous zone. Making her crazy. Making her hot. And, most of all, making her forget the horrific situation that had trapped them together.

"Joan?" His lips brushed her ear, and she shivered, the contact sending a million electrical flurries skittering over her body. She realized she'd gotten lost in her fantasies, mixing the reality of his touch with the meanderings of her mind.

"Yes?" Her voice was breathless, and she had to force the single word out.

"Tell me. What do you want?" He stroked her leg as he spoke, finding the sensitive area behind her knee.

Joan opened her mouth to answer, barely able to form thoughts, much less actual words. She shifted until she could look him in the eye, the movement causing his hands to rub up against her waist. The heat burning in her body was reflected right back at her in his eyes. ''You,'' she said. ''Right now, I want you.''

BRYCE HAD EXPECTED her answer. Joan wouldn't last a day in the wilds of Wall Street; her eyes gave too much away. But what he *hadn't* expected was the overwhelming rush of relief when she spoke that one word— ''You.''

She wanted him, just as hundreds of other women did. But never before had he felt he'd be risking severe disappointment if a woman walked away from him. And it would have been more than just a blow to his ego. That, he could handle. With Joan, there was more at stake. Her aggressiveness coupled with her sense of self intrigued him. Hell, everything about her intrigued him, including the way she filled out that dress. He had no intention of starting up something that would last long-term, but, right then, only Joan filled his thoughts.

He told himself he simply wanted to protect her, to hold and caress her. But it was more than that. So much more, in fact, that he didn't want to think about it. The woman messed with his head in a way he'd never experienced before. And the sensation was both unnerving and enticing.

She was looking up at him, her bright blue eyes hiding a hint of a question—had she said the wrong thing? He didn't answer out loud. Instead, he tugged her close, so that she was no longer balancing one leg on the sofa, but was standing right in front of him.

She released a little breath of surprise, and for some reason the sound turned him on even more than her earlier demand for him had. She was lost in the moment, lost in a haze of desire. *For him.* And he didn't intend to disappoint.

He closed his mouth over hers, delighted when her lips parted automatically so he could deepen the kiss. He'd wanted to kiss her since the first moment they'd locked eyes in the bookstore, and now he made up for lost time, his tongue exploring and teasing as his hands explored her body.

One hand continued to cup her waist, but with his other hand he stroked her leg. Her skin was soft, and his fingers grazed over her calf, her knee, and then up her thigh. She'd come to his apartment in a come-hither dress, and Bryce thought she looked absolutely edible. The dress hit her thigh at about the same place as the skirt she'd been wearing at the store. He'd fantasized then about the delights waiting for him under that short bit of material. Now he intended to find out.

With the palm of his hand, he stroked her bare

thigh, sliding his hand around to the soft skin on the inside of her leg. A low moan settled in her throat, and she slid her own hands down to his ass, silently urging him toward her.

He was rock-hard, and he had to draw on every ounce of willpower in his body not to toss that skirt up, lay her back over the couch, rip off her panties, and sink deep inside her.

But no. He wanted to take this slow. Wanted to keep them both on edge for as long as possible.

After all, as far as he knew, they really did have all the time in the world.

She broke the kiss, murmuring soft words of protest when he resisted her efforts to press their bodies together.

"Trust me," he said. He wanted distance. Not too much, just enough so that he had room to explore her body. Press too close, and he lost the ability to maneuver. And right then, Bryce wanted to slide his hands over her body almost as much as he wanted to sink deep inside her.

"You're torturing me," she said.

"Payback," he murmured. "Your punishment for spying on me."

"If this is punishment," she said, "I'm dying to know what you'd do to me if I did something really bad."

He grinned, but didn't answer. Instead, he skimmed his palm up her side, noting with pleasure the slight tremble that shook her body. His hands grazed the soft skin just under her arms, bare from the cut of the dress. With his thumb, he reached out, letting the pad tease her erect nipple. Joan closed her eyes, her head tilted back, and Bryce placed a gentle kiss in the soft spot between her neck and collarbone.

"More," she whispered.

"Shhh," he said, then brushed a kiss over her lips. "My payback, my rules."

She whimpered in response, a soft, needy sound, and once again Bryce almost lost control.

He didn't, though. Not yet. Not until he couldn't stand it anymore.

He moved his hand, and lowered his mouth to her breast, suckling her through the thin, purple material. With his other hand, he returned his attention to her thigh, stroking up until the tips of his fingers brushed against the lace of her panties.

She shifted her stance, widening her legs to give him better access. Bryce smiled. The woman knew what she wanted, and damned if Bryce didn't want the same thing.

"This?" he whispered, tracing the pad of his finger over the elastic band between her crotch and her thigh.

"Yes," she murmured, then shook her head. "I mean no. More." She forced the words out. "Bryce, please."

"More," he repeated, feigning confusion. "You

mean like this?'' He cupped his palm, then stroked his fingertips over her satin-covered mound.

Her panties were damp, and she bucked against his hand, an involuntary movement as her body demanded even more.

He shifted their positions until his legs straddled her, and her opposite thigh was pressed against him. His erection rubbed against her leg, and now he moaned in pleasure, his body tightening as her sweet heat stroked him.

''Bryce.'' His name was a whisper, but it was also a demand. He slipped just the tip of his finger under the elastic, barely grazing her flesh, and nowhere near the sweet spot where he knew she craved his touch.

''Like that?'' he said.

''Dammit, Bryce. Touch me,'' she said, her voice low and delicious. ''Touch me or you're *really* going to learn about payback.''

He laughed, but complied. He'd been torturing himself as much as her, and the truth was he wanted her. Wanted to watch as she melted under his touch. Wanted to look into her eyes as he made her come.

Roughly, he pushed the crotch of her panties aside, then slid his fingers through her slick, wet curls until he found her center. Her breathing was uneven, punctuated by low murmurs of ''yes'' and ''please.''

He didn't disappoint. He slipped his forefinger and index finger inside her, cupping her sex with his palm as he stroked her. He felt himself harden as he continued the erotic rhythm, sliding in and out in slow, deep movements designed to take her right to the edge.

"Do you like that?"

"Oh, God, yes." A pause, and then, "But what part of 'more' don't you understand?"

Her words worked a magic on him, and he couldn't stand it anymore. Enough with the slow teases and the slow builds. He wanted her, and he wanted her now.

He shifted them, taking her in a deep, passionate kiss. At the same time, he urged them, moving as one, across the room until she was pressed up against the pillar that marked the end of the living area and the beginning of the small kitchenette.

Her breath came fast, her eyes widening in both question and excitement.

"More," he said simply.

A smile touched her lips. "About damn time."

Her fingers reached for the waistband of his sweats, nimbly untying the knot that held up the pants. She released the drawstring, and the garment slid down over his hips. He hadn't worn underwear, and now the cool air acted as an enticing counterpoint to the heat generated between the two of them.

She reached down to cup his balls, then stroked him. His body rocked, and it was everything he could do not to come right then, as her touch sent about a million volts of pure electricity racing through him.

Gently, he tugged her hand away. "Not yet," he said. "Not unless you want a different ending to this show than the one I had planned."

"Couldn't have that," she murmured. She swung her arm around his neck, this time taking him in a kiss that she controlled. Her hands stroked his body, slipping under his T-shirt to stroke his chest, roaming around his back and then down to cup his ass. She was wild and determined and knew exactly what she wanted, and her touch turned Bryce on even more than he already was.

"Joan," he said, the one word both a demand and a plea. He pressed her back against the pillar, his free hand groping on the counter for his wallet. He found it, then fumbled for a condom as she shifted against him, her soft movements as demanding as words. He slipped it on, then moved closer, lifting her skirt with one hand as he grabbed the band of her panties with the other. He started to tug them down, but she shook her head.

"Rip them," she demanded. And when he did, she arched her back, her nipples hard against the soft folds of her dress, her expression one of pure delight.

Right then, Bryce knew he couldn't take it anymore. He pushed closer, the tip of his erection pressing against her and his hips moving in a sensual rhythm. But it wasn't enough. And with one bold movement, he clutched her waist and lifted her, then pulled her down onto his rock-hard shaft.

She moaned, an erotic sound of pure pleasure, and arched her back. With her legs, she grabbed hold, locking her ankles behind him as she clutched him around the neck.

Her eyes were closed while she rode him, but Bryce kept his eyes open, wanting to see her face, wanting to watch as her body took him in and as she pushed toward the edge.

He lifted her easily, thrusting her down in a practiced rhythm, impaling her on him, every motion designed to bring her—and him—right to the cusp and over. Her teeth grazed her lips; her eyes glazed with passion. And through it all, he watched her, the flush on her cheeks, the erotic curve of her neck, the delicate line of her collar. But there was nothing delicate about her movements. She matched him thrust for thrust, lifting her body and then slamming back down as the pressure built and built in both of them.

He was close, so very close, but he fought release, wanting to come with her, to feel her body tighten around him and milk him dry. He closed his eyes, fighting the sensations.

But then she gasped, and that was all it took. He was lost, unable to hold back any longer. And when his release came, wave after wave of delirious pleasure, it was so strong it almost knocked him off his feet.

Joan trembled in his arms, the muscles that sheathed him clenching and unclenching as she cried out, a series of small ''ohs'' and then his name. *His name.* It sounded so right to hear it drift from her lips.

She melted against him, her legs dropping to the ground to provide some needed balance. His own legs gave out, and he urged her down to the ground, curling her up close against him as they lay there half-naked on the hotel's oriental tapestry rug.

They lay there, breathing deep, until she tossed her bare leg over his, then leaned up on an elbow to face him. ''Well,'' she said with a slow grin, ''that was a nice first course.''

''First course?'' he said.

''Well, appetizer, then.''

He laughed. ''In that case, if we're stuck up here for longer than two hours, I think I may be a dead man.''

''Nah,'' she said. ''But I guarantee you'll get quite a workout.''

''Good,'' he said. ''I haven't been to the gym in ages.''

Her finger traced a pattern on his chest. ''I find that hard to believe.''

Since he went to the gym three times a week, he didn't argue. ''Let's just say it's been a long time since I've had such a...thorough...workout.''

''Fair enough,'' she said. She plucked at her dress, then looked down at her legs, one still clad in a stocking, the other bare. ''I'm something of a mess,'' she said.

"Sweetheart," he said. "I think you look beautiful."

She laughed, a bubbly, delighted sound. "Bryce, you say the sweetest things. But next time," she added, "I think I'd like to do it naked."

BY THE TIME Donovan had gotten half a block from the Monteleone, the hostage rescue team was in place and going full force. The area was crawling with activity, lit up like Yankee Stadium, just as he knew it would be. The staging area where the team had set up had a view of the hotel, but wasn't so close it would spook the gunman.

About fifty meters away, he could see an area that had been set up for the media, and the department liaison was standing in front of the cameras, looking more cool and collected than Donovan ever did on the rare occasions he had to talk to the press.

He waved over a uniformed officer, who tucked a clipboard under his arm and hurried to Donovan's side. "Where's Fisk?" The officer pointed toward a cadre of men gathered around the portable com center. A burly fellow Donovan didn't recognize stepped aside at that moment, revealing Lieutenant Fisk's wiry frame and prematurely gray hair. Donovan lingered on the sidelines until Fisk finished briefing his team, then meandered up to his academy classmate.

"Donovan," Fisk said, looking up from an enlarged map of the area. "What brings you down here?"

"I've got a friend in there. Thought I'd come make sure you guys were doing your jobs." His tone was light, and he knew his buddy wouldn't take offense. Fisk ran the hostage rescue team, and his team was the best in the business.

Fisk's face darkened. "Your friend was in the kitchen?"

Donovan shook his head. "No, no. She's fine. She's in the hotel."

Fisk's brow furrowed. "Name?"

"Joan. Joan Benetti."

Fisk rifled through a few sheets on a clipboard, then lifted a hand, waving over one of his men. "Is this list updated?"

The officer glanced over it and nodded. "Yes, sir."

Fisk looked up at Donovan. "We've evacuated the building. Your friend's not on the list."

"Impossible," Donovan said. "I talked to her myself less than an hour ago."

"If she's in there," Fisk said, "she's in the penthouse. There's a private elevator to that floor, and we decided not to evacuate. Under the circumstances, it was just too risky."

Donovan licked his lips. He had no idea what Joan would be doing at the penthouse at the Monteleone, but that had to be where she was. "What about her friend? Angie Tate. She clocked out before the gunman arrived. Has anyone heard from her?''

''Tate?'' Fisk repeated. He tilted his head down, looking at Donovan from under bushy eyebrows. ''Angela Tate?''

A finger of dread eased down between Donovan's shoulder blades. ''Yeah. That's her.''

''I'm sorry, buddy,'' Fisk said. ''She's one of the hostages.''

7

FISK HAD TO GO make some statement to the media and oversee the rest of his team, so it was a while before Donovan was able to get his friend alone again to find out the details.

"I decided not to tell Joan," he said. "There's no sense worrying her when she can't do a damn thing where she is."

Fisk nodded. "I agree."

"Good," Donovan said. "Because I told her a little white lie."

Fisk's bushy eyebrows lifted. "Oh?"

Donovan shrugged, feeling a little guilty, but not much. He knew Joan. She took things to heart. Plus, she was a sweet kid and she didn't deserve to spend God knows how long trapped in a hotel room worrying about what was going on below. "I just called Joanie's cell phone," he admitted. "I told her everything is under control, that we've confirmed the hostages are safe, and that we're doing the negotiating thing, but that takes a while. I told her it looks real positive and none of our psych guys expect the perp to hurt anyone."

Fisk just stared at him. "You told her that?"

"Yup."

After a second, Fisk nodded. "Well, considering my plan is to get everyone out unharmed, I can't chew you out too much." He half grinned. "Even if your announcement was premature." Fisk tapped his clipboard. "You said she's Angela Tate's friend?"

"That's right."

"We're sending an officer to Tate's sister's apartment. I'll make sure the officer recommends discretion to the sister, just in case she talks to Joan over a cell phone."

"Thanks," Donovan said. "I appreciate it." He looked around at the scene. "So who *is* negotiating?" Donovan asked. The team always had one negotiator take the lead in any hostage situation.

"Wilson," Fisk said. "But nobody's talking right now. Our guy is spooked. We're letting him take his time. Meanwhile, we're trying to confirm the snipers and the other gunmen." Donovan must have frowned, because Fisk went on. "So far, we've got no indication there's anyone but him down there." Fisk shrugged. "Not that it matters. One gunman or twenty, our initial strategy isn't going to change much. But the snipers..."

Donovan nodded. "We need to know."

"Exactly." Fisk sucked down some coffee from a cardboard cup, then made a face. "Shit's ice-cold." He shook his head, getting back on topic. "Point is, we haven't got any confirmation on the snipers. But nothing to confirm they're not there, either.''

''Can I help?''

Fisk laughed. ''I don't think the homicides in this city have ground to a halt because of a hostage situation. Don't worry. We've got it under control.''

Donovan nodded. He knew that the team was on top of it. And the truth was, now was not the time to be making waves by jumping into the middle of an investigation that wasn't in his job description. He was too new to homicide—fresh off of sex crimes—to be making waves.

Fisk nodded toward the news vans littering the area. ''We haven't released the hostage list to the media yet,'' he said. ''We're contacting relatives first.''

''Makes sense,'' Donovan said.

''We're waiting to release the identity of the penthouse occupant, too,'' Fisk said. He frowned. ''Considering the media frenzy, though, I'm wondering if we shouldn't do it sooner—before some overeager reporter grabs onto the story and runs.''

Donovan shook his head, not understanding. ''The penthouse? What story? I thought you said Joan was safe. If there's—''

''No, no. We have no reason to believe there's any risk to anyone remaining in the penthouse. I just meant that considering who she's with, it's going to be big news.''

Donovan blinked. ''Why? Who's she with?''

"Bryce Worthington," Fisk said.

Donovan let out a low whistle. Fisk was right. The media was going to be all over that. "That's why you didn't evacuate the penthouse," he said. "Worthington."

Fisk nodded. "A man in his position must have a lot of enemies. If there are snipers, I don't want him walking out into the middle of them."

Donovan nodded. Intellectually, he agreed with Fisk's assessment. More importantly, his gut told him that Worthington's existence at the scene of a hostage crisis was more than just coincidence.

He prayed that as long as Worthington and Joan stayed inside, fifteen floors away from the gunman and his snipers, they'd be safe. As safe as possible, anyway.

No matter what, though, the media was going to be all over this. As for Joan, he couldn't help but wonder if the press would focus on the singular question running through Donovan's head—what the hell was a girl like Joanie doing with the likes of Worthington?

CLIVE BALANCED the rifle across his knees, keeping his handgun ready at the same time. He'd ushered his hostages into the dining room, and now he was at one of the tables, his gaze surveying the seven cowering insurance policies. Their eyes were bloodshot, their faces drawn and scared. Clive didn't care. He needed to get out of here, and it was their own fault, anyway.

They'd been in the wrong place at the wrong time, and they were stupid enough not to fight back. He wasn't even going to kill them, and they *still* didn't fight. *He* would have fought. That's what you had to do. You had to fight for survival. That's why he was going after Worthington. Payback. For him, and for Emily.

She'd fought. Oh, yeah. She'd fought. But without the insurance, it wasn't a battle she could win.

Now Clive was fighting for her.

But damned if his plan hadn't gotten all screwed up. Now he had to focus. Focus hard. He had to get out of this mess alive. He needed another shot at Worthington, and if he got caught, the bastard would get off, never paying for his crimes.

With a sigh, he let his gaze drift over the huddled hostages. The police had evacuated the building hours ago, setting up a perimeter and treating him with kid gloves. As long as he was stuck, at least his hostages were keeping him alive. As long as the cops thought he might blow one of their brains out, they wouldn't rush the hotel with guns blazing.

That, at least, gave Clive time to work up a plan.

The cops would, however, keep calling him every hour asking for his demands. Right now, it was almost two in the morning. They'd be calling again soon.

Two minutes. Three. The phone at the hostess station rang. Right on the money.

Clive got up, keeping his gun trained on the hostages as he crossed the room. He picked up the handset. "Yeah?"

"Are you ready to talk terms?"

"I told you already," he whispered, knowing that would make it more difficult for them to identify his voice. "We got nothing to talk about."

"Will you release just one hostage then? A show of good faith."

Clive squinted, looking at the hostages huddled together in the dark. He'd ripped the tablecloths into strips to bind their wrists and ankles. As long as they were there and quiet, they were insurance. He wasn't about to let one go. "I'll talk it over with my team," he whispered.

"Can we talk to the hostages again?"

Clive ran a hand through his hair. During their first call, he'd had each hostage shout their name into the phone, just so the cops knew he was serious. He wasn't going through that nonsense again.

"No," he said. "But they're alive. Listen." He held the phone out. "Say something to the nice policemen."

The hostages shouted, their voices filling the thick silence. Clive waved the gun, then made a slicing noise across his throat. They shut up.

"Hostages," he whispered. "Just like you asked for."

He heard a murmur on the other end of the line, as

if someone was talking with their hand over the microphone. Then the contact officer came back on the line. ''We'll call you again in an hour.''

''Fine,'' he said. ''Do anything else, though, and I start killing these people.''

CRAZY. That's what it was. That despite the situation she was in—stuck in a hotel where a madman was holding hostages—Joan could actually feel...well, wonderful. Stiff and sore and spent...but absolutely wonderful.

They'd moved to the sofa, and she was lying across it, her feet in Bryce's lap. She was still in the dress, but she'd taken off the stray stocking, and now he was gently stroking her legs, the touch keeping her body humming. Warm and comfortable, she stretched like a cat, practically purring with satisfaction. ''Wonderful,'' she murmured. ''I feel absolutely wonderful.''

Bryce chuckled. ''I'd like to think it was all me, but I know that phone call from Donovan helped.''

Joan tilted her head, smiling at him. ''It just lifts a huge weight knowing that everything is okay. That those poor people are going to be fine, and all we're doing is waiting for the negotiators to do their job for them to get their happy ending.''

Donovan's call had gone a long way toward easing both her guilt for having such a wonderful time with

Bryce, and her fear that somehow the horrible situation below them would trickle up the stairs.

"I know," he said as he scooted toward her, so that her thighs were now resting on his legs. Then he reached out and stroked her cheek, the rough pads of his fingers exceedingly gentle.

His hands had surprised her. She'd expected the soft, manicured hands of a man who spent his life behind a desk, counting his dollars from afar. But his fingers were rough, his hands calloused, and the dichotomy was unbelievably erotic. She closed her eyes, soaking up his touch.

"Now we wait," he said. "Think you can handle waiting here, all alone, with me?"

There was a tease in his voice, and she answered just as playfully. "Well, I don't know…."

"I'll make it easy on you," Bryce said. "Just pretend that we're snowed in at a villa in the Swiss Alps having a decadent time."

"Well, the decadent part I can handle. But the rest…" She laughed. "I'm not sure my imagination is that good. I mean, it's close to a hundred degrees outside, and I've never even been out of the country, much less to the Alps."

"Really?" A flash of surprise crossed his face. "In your business, I would have thought you made frequent trips to London and Paris."

Joan stifled a frown. Already she was caught in her own lie. "I'm looking forward to that part of the business, actually, but I just, uh, came on board recently. I joined forces with Ronnie because of my academic expertise in the area.'' Even as she spoke she cursed herself. She should just come clean. After all, it wasn't as if he could kick her out. But she'd already told him she co-owned the store, and surely a business owner would have more experience than her résumé showed.

He cocked an eyebrow. ''Interesting. So you have a Ph.D.?''

''Yeah,'' she said, digging her hole deeper and hoping he wouldn't ask her any more questions since she knew neither the ins and outs of getting a Ph.D. nor the proper lingo for joining a partnership. Buying in? Getting hired? Coming on board had seemed as good a guess as any. Hopefully she hadn't completely blown it.

''And Ronnie?''

''Oh, she's fabulous at everything. She grew up in the business. She can practically sniff out rare books. You should see some of the treasures she's found at ratty old flea markets.''

''Really? I love ratty old flea markets myself.''

She frowned. ''You do?'' She loved them, too, but somehow digging around amidst the junk searching for a jewel wasn't an activity she would have placed in the top ten of A Billionaire's Favorite Things to Do. Then again, she never would have pictured a man

like Bryce Worthington in sweatpants, but she had to admit she liked what she saw.

"I hit a few flea markets now and then. You should see some of the pieces I've collected over the years." His mouth twitched. "I even have a wall hanging made from old Texas license plates. Very retro chic." He leaned in, almost as if he was sharing an investment tip. "I paid twenty bucks at a flea market in Kyle. A steal."

"Kyle?"

"A small town outside of Austin. I'm from Texas."

"Oh," she said. The realization that he lived somewhere else depressed her at the same time that it erased her guilt. There was no chance that anything permanent would ever develop between the two of them, so while they were tossed together by fate, she could be anyone she wanted to be. And at the moment, she wanted to be a well-read academic knowledgeable about all things erotic. "So what are you doing in Manhattan? The deposition? The gallery opening?"

"All on the agenda," he admitted, "but mostly I came here for a deal," he said. "By the time I get out of here, though, the whole thing will probably have collapsed."

She thought about asking what he meant, but the truth was that she didn't give two hoots about the world of Wall Street, and listening to him explain the details would probably bore her to tears. At the same time, she didn't want to seem uninterested. They'd slept together—hopefully would again—and she didn't want him to think that was *all* that was on her mind.

"So what is it you do?" she finally asked. "I mean, in a nutshell. For those of us who are corporately challenged."

"I started out buying and selling buildings. Now I buy and sell companies."

"Oh. Well, that's cool."

"Cool," he repeated. "Yes, I guess it is." He gave her hand a gentle squeeze. "You're an interesting woman, Joan Benetti."

She laughed, but her stomach was twisting into knots, the neurons firing again in response to his hand on hers. "I bet you say that to all the women who break into your hotel room."

"Not at all," he countered. "Only the ones who see me naked."

She rolled her eyes. "Well, in that case, I'm glad I'm interesting. Because I definitely enjoyed the view."

He trailed his hand up and down her leg, the movements slow and sensuous. "Of course, this does put a crimp in my plans for the evening."

Joan licked her lips, every bit of energy in her body focused on where his fingertips touched. "Oh?" She had to force the word out.

"I'd planned to spend hours convincing you to let me touch you." The hand stroked up, grazing her bare skin under her skirt. "To let me explore all your intimate secrets." Back down to her knee. "Your most sensitive places." Up again, but not nearly as high as she wanted.

Joan closed her eyes, silently willing his fingers higher, wanting him to touch her just a little. To quench the pulsing burn between her thighs. She was like Louisa in *Fanny Hill*, insatiable. Desperate for a man's touch. Only for Joan, she lusted after only one man—Bryce. With Bryce, she knew she could be sated. And, oh, how she would enjoy getting there.

Once again she licked her lips. "And now?" she asked.

His smile was pure sin. "Now I don't think you need any more convincing."

His hand skimmed higher, and she gasped. "No, I have to say you've made your point." She sounded breathless to her own ears. "Although..."

Bryce laughed. "Yes?" He trailed off, and at the same time he lifted his fingers from her flesh. Her body mourned the loss of contact, and she opened her eyes, staring at him in accusation. He shrugged.

"About that book you wanted to buy..." She fought a smile. "Now that you've admitted your ulterior motive, tell me the truth. Do you even *have* a collection?"

"I'm starting one tonight," he said, then raised a hand as though in oath. "I swear."

"Uh-huh." She crossed her arms over her chest and tried to look serious.

"No, it's true. And I think I'll be starting my collection with a lovely little title called *The Pleasures of a Young Woman.*"

She laughed. "Fair enough. And since we're being perfectly honest, I suppose I should tell you that I had a bit of an ulterior motive in *accepting* your dinner reservation."

"I'm intrigued."

"Information," she said, stopping her hand just shy of the bulge in his pants. "I was hoping to extract information."

He nodded toward her hand. "If that's the method you intended to use, I predict the utmost success."

"Good," she said. "I wouldn't want the job to be too hard."

"Maybe not the job," he said. "But..."

She laughed. "Touché. Sometimes harder is better."

"What kind of information?"

"Business information."

He half frowned, a flicker of interest tamping out the expression of playfulness. "Go on."

"The store could be doing better," she said. "And, uh, I'm trying to convince Ronnie to, um, increase my what-do-you-call-it? Ownership interest."

"And you thought I could help?"

"You seem like the kind of guy who has a handle on the business world." She shrugged. "And when you offered to buy three volumes, well, I knew you were the kind of guy who could help out the bottom line."

"And now? I assume you still want me to buy the three volumes?"

"Oh, yeah. Definitely." She grinned. "But I had also planned to ply you with wine at dinner and ask you lots of questions. You know, about marketing and balance sheets and stuff like that."

He nodded, his expression serious. "Basic dinner-time conversation."

"Sure. I mean, I've just got my little degree in literature. You must have MBAs and all that kind of stuff hanging all over your walls."

"Oh, yeah. It's hard to walk through my office I've got so many diplomas and certificates." His grin was back, and she knew that he was making fun of her. She didn't care. He had information that she wanted. For that, she was happy to come across as a little naïve. Especially when she was naïve.

"All right," he continued. "This lesson's free. We're in the negotiation phase of the relationship. We each have something the other wants, and the trick is to satisfy us both without putting too much on the table, or giving up too much in the process."

She nodded. "Right."

"I'll make this one easy," he said. "I'll give you your lessons. I'll tell you everything you want to know. But I want a few lessons of my own in trade."

She squinted. "What kind of lessons?"

"Exactly what I told you at the store." He reached over, then plucked *Pleasures* off the coffee table. "I'm intrigued. I'd like to learn more." His gaze met hers, passion burning in his eyes. "And at the moment, I have the perfect teacher at my beck and call."

"Oh." Joan licked her lips as his words soaked in. *"Oh!"* She pulled her legs up to her chest and hugged her knees. Her brow furrowed as she considered his words. Erotica lessons for a man like Bryce…it was enough to take her breath away.

Only she didn't want to just walk him through the literature. Oh no. If she was going to play teacher, she wanted it to be a wholly enriching learning experience.

For four years now, she'd spent six days a week surrounded by erotic prose and enticing images. When the store was busy, she could turn it off, block it out. But during the slow times…

Well, her imagination had a tendency to wander. And the meandering path it took often led down scenarios similar to those she'd read about in the break room. Joan was no slouch in the men department, but she'd yet to find a man with whom she wanted to share those erotic fantasies, with whom she really wanted to push the envelope.

But with Bryce... Oh, with Bryce she wanted to share all that and more.

"Joan?"

"All right," she said, looking up at him. She straightened her legs, resting them across his as she reached for her wine. "I'll teach you about the erotica," she agreed, "but we have to use my methods." She drew in a breath, summoning her courage. "I've been reading this stuff for years and it's...well, titillating. But your imagination can only go so far, you know?"

"So..." He left the sentence hanging, forcing her to spell it out.

She lifted her chin. "If you teach me about running a business, I'll teach you about erotica. But my lessons will be hands-on. *Very* hands-on." She cocked her head, hoping she looked self-assured. "Think you can handle those terms?"

"Sweetheart," he said with a grin, "I think we have a deal."

8

BRYCE WASN'T CERTAIN why Joan wanted him to believe she had a Ph.D., but he was almost certain that she didn't have a master's, much less a doctorate. He could be wrong, of course, but he didn't think so. He'd spent too many years on the opposite side of the negotiating table with people who wanted him to believe that they held more cards than they did.

Joan had hesitated over her words, fidgeted with her hands, pulled her legs and arms in so that she was no longer touching him, and—the kicker—instead of meeting his eyes, her gaze had drifted off to the left. A sure sign that she was engaging in some massive fabrication.

The deception disturbed him, hit just a little too close to home. His mother had spent years living one huge lie. Pretending to have a part-time job, when in reality she had a part-time lover. A lover who later became her husband. She'd lied to Bryce and his father, and Bryce had never forgiven her.

Even so, he wasn't inclined to quibble about Joan's fabrication. Her true educational background was no concern of his. The woman might set his body thrumming and his blood pumping, but that didn't mean that Bryce anticipated any future beyond the time he had in New York. What Bryce had told Leo was true—he wasn't looking for a woman. Not a permanent one, anyway.

So Joan could pretend to be whoever she wanted. And if she wanted to be a Ph.D., then who was he to complain? Especially since he was going to reap such a magnificent benefit from her supposedly hard-earned expertise. Even now, her words seemed to linger in the air—*hands-on.* Oh yeah. If she wanted to play the teacher, then Bryce was more than willing to play the role of student.

Willing? Hell, who was he kidding? The word was desperate. They'd been sitting on this damn couch in postcoital bliss for an eternity. The proximity had fired his blood. No curling up in a haze of exhausted sleep for him. No, he was already rock hard and he wanted her again. And again. And again after that.

Considering her reaction to his touch—not to mention her little teaching proposition—she wanted him, too.

He reached over to the coffee table for the bottle of wine, then topped off their glasses. "So, tell me, professor. What exactly do you plan to teach me?"

"Funny you should ask," she said. "I was just pondering my lesson plan."

As he passed her the wineglass, their fingers brushed, even that slight contact shooting straight to his groin. The circumstances, the sex and the woman herself were all working on him, sending a surge of desire through his body that he had no intention of ignoring. He was running on sexual arousal and adrenaline, and it was time to get their school for scandal underway.

As she took a sip, he apologized. "I should offer you something to eat, but there's not much here."

She arched her neck, peering over the couch toward the kitchenette.

"Some olives," he said, answering her unasked question, "a bag of Famous Amos cookies, another bottle of wine—two, actually—a bottle of vodka, a gallon of orange juice, and a box of chocolates I bought for my attorney's secretary."

She laughed. "I knew some millionaires were frugal," she said. "But that seems like a hell of a way to keep your grocery bill low."

"Cute." He brushed the tip of her nose with his forefinger. "I never bother to have the hotel stock the kitchen when I stay here. I'm usually dining out on business or too busy to care."

"Thus the nightly room service."

"Exactly. It ensures I get a little nourishment at the end of the day."

"I don't mind the lack of food," she said, placing her glass back on the coffee table. She licked her lips, the simple gesture unbelievably erotic. "I plan to get my fill of you."

Her words washed over him like a caress, bringing him even closer to the edge. With a low groan, he slid his hand over hers, twining their fingers. Then he lifted their joined hands to his mouth and pressed a kiss to the top of her forefinger. "I'm ready for class to begin."

She shivered, a slight tremor that brought him tremendous satisfaction. "Soon," she said, closing her eyes. He brought the tip of her finger into his mouth, his tongue spiraling around her soft skin. Her breath hitched. "Very soon," she whispered.

His teeth grazed lightly over her finger as he slipped the digit free, then pressed a kiss to her palm. "Good," he said. "Just so you know, I always ace my classes."

"Is that a fact?" She let her gaze trail over him, Bryce's body reacting as if it were her fingers, rather than her eyes, that had danced over his skin. With her gaze trained firmly on his, she picked up her glass. She took a sip, then ran her tongue over her lips, the gesture designed to seduce. "Nice wine," she said.

"I'm glad you approve."

She finished off the glass, then poured another. She took a sip and then leaned forward, plucking a grape from the tray of fruit and cheese. She pursed her lips, drawing the grape in as Bryce wondered if he would explode right then and there.

"If you're trying to drive me crazy," he said, "you're succeeding."

Her grin was wide and mischievous as she reached for another grape. "Busted."

"Hmmm." He sent her a mock glare. "Better be careful. Good food, good wine. I don't want you falling asleep on me. It's already after three. And I don't appreciate deal-welshers."

One delicate eyebrow lifted above the frame of her glasses. "Welshing?" She trailed a fingertip down his arm, leaving a path of heat in its wake. "Can't have that."

"I should hope not."

"Never fear. I've been doing the New York club scene for years. If I'm in bed before four, it's an early night."

"Either that or you're not in bed alone."

He hid his grin as her cheeks bloomed to that adorable shade of pink once again.

"I go to bed alone more than you'd think," she said. She looked him up and down, as if taking measure of his various assets. "I'm extremely discriminating."

"I'm honored," he said.

"You should be." He could tell she was trying to keep her expression serious, but the twitch at the corner of her mouth betrayed her. "Besides," she added. "Sleep isn't necessarily a bad thing, even where erotica is concerned. In fact, it's our first lesson."

He frowned. The conversation had definitely turned in an unexpected direction.

His confusion must have reflected on his face, because she laughed, then brushed a kiss over his lips. The brief kiss was almost chaste, but it made a promise that was anything but pure. "Trust me," she whispered. "I'm an expert, remember?"

"How could I forget? I'm counting the minutes until you share your expertise." Counting the minutes? That was an understatement. His entire body was thrumming with anticipation.

"I'm glad to hear it," she said. She leaned back in the cushions, the epitome of a woman who had all the time in the world. "So what about my tat?"

He blinked, wondering if somehow he'd missed an entirely new euphemism. "What?"

"Well, assuming this goes as expected, I think it's fair to say you're going to get a bit of tit. My tits, to be exact." She raised her eyebrows. "So when do I get my tat?"

He laughed. The woman definitely kept him on his toes. "Sweetheart, you can have your tat whenever you want it."

She leaned forward, pressing her palm against his crotch with just enough pressure to edge him toward insanity. "I'll keep that in mind," she said, then brushed a kiss across his cheek before retreating to her end of the couch. Bryce shook his head. He'd never been a big fan of boxing, but he knew a technical knockout when he saw one, and Joan had just laid one on him, and good.

"My *tat,*" she said, "is in your head, not in your pants." Her eyes dropped down to the telltale bulge under the gray fleece of his sweatpants. "But don't worry, we won't let that go to waste."

"I'm so glad to hear it."

"Waste not, want not," she said. "That's what my grammie always says."

"A wise woman, your grammie."

She lifted an eyebrow. "Well?"

"You'll get your tat in the morning," he said. "Business theory is more appropriate during the daylight hours. Whereas our current topic—"

"Sleep," she said. "Definitely a nighttime activity."

"Sleep," he repeated, feigning disappointment. He didn't know what she had planned, but he wasn't really worried.

"Are you familiar with Havelock Ellis?" she asked.

He shook his head. The name was familiar, but he couldn't place it.

"He studied sex," she said. "A sexologist, I guess you'd call him. He didn't actually write erotica, but we have a few volumes of his works in the store because he studied sexual response, and wrote some really interesting stuff on erotic symbolism." She licked her lips. "That's part of lesson number one. Symbols."

Bryce nodded, watching Joan with fascination. She

might not have the degree, but she definitely had the information. She still had the aura of a sultry sex kitten, but there was an intellectual component now, too, and he wouldn't have been at all surprised if she'd reached into her purse and pulled out tortoiseshell glasses to replace the lavender ones, along with a laser pointer and a thick pad of notes.

"Ellis said there were three kinds of erotic symbols. First, parts of the body—like feet, earlobes and other erogenous zones. Second, there are inanimate objects." She reached over to the coffee table and plucked his tie up from beside the tray, then draped it over her neck. "Like this," she said, as she slowly pulled it free, as though in an erotic striptease. "Understand?"

"I think I've got it," Bryce said, concentrating on the swell of her breasts under the soft purple material.

"The last one is acts and attitudes."

He shook his head, not certain what she meant.

"Things like spanking or being spanked. Or fooling around in one of those padded swings." She paused, thoughtfully. "I've never tried that...." she added, her voice trailing off.

"Too bad we don't have a swing," he said. "We could fill that gap in your education right now."

"Yes, too bad."

"None of that sounds very sleep-inducing," he said.

"No, it wouldn't be. But my point is that I think

Ellis missed one. A big one. My thesis is that there's a wealth of erotica found in sleep.'' She licked her lips. ''There's something very erotic about watching your lover—or even just some person you're trapped in a building with—sleep.''

''Or just watching them,'' Bryce said, cutting a glance toward the screen behind which she'd hidden.

''Very true.'' She grinned. ''But voyeurism, while related, is another lesson altogether.''

''So you weren't really hiding back there,'' he said. ''You were researching.''

''Absolutely,'' she said, her expression serious. ''Voyeurism with a higher purpose.''

''Higher than sex? I find that hard to believe.''

She smacked him across the knee with the back of her hand. ''A little respect, please,'' she said. ''This is serious business.''

He looked at his knee. ''Slapping,'' he said. ''Your friend Havelock would find symbolism there.'' He cocked his head to the side, narrowing his eyes to stare at her. ''Ms. Benetti,'' he said, ''all these little symbols, these unspoken innuendos…are you trying to seduce me?''

''Trying and succeeding,'' she said, then stood up. He expected her to move close to him. Instead she took a step away, backing out from between the sofa and the coffee table.

''Going somewhere?''

''As a matter of fact, yes.'' She nodded toward the

bedroom. ''Sleep,'' she said. ''I presume you want me to keep up my stamina.''

He raised an eyebrow. ''I thought you were the woman who shut down even the hippest of New York clubs.''

''True. But we're not clubbing. And I need my beauty rest. Especially if I'm going to be clearheaded tomorrow when you give me my business lesson.''

''Don't hold your breath, sweetheart. Without tit, you're not getting tat.''

She reached down into her oversize purse, then pulled out a single volume. She flipped through it, finally marking a place with her finger. ''Frank Harris,'' she said as she passed him the book.

He took it, replacing her finger with his as a page marker.

''This is lesson number one. You study that...and then you tell me what you learned.'' She brushed a light kiss along his cheek, the gesture filled with erotic promises, then walked toward the bedroom.

Bryce watched her go, both bemused and bewildered. At least, that is, until he opened the book to the marked page. He only had to read a few lines before bewilderment was pushed aside by arousal, anticipation and just a hint of jealousy directed at the couple described on the pages.

The woman was sleeping, wearing nothing but a thin silk chemise with the covers tossed aside in deference to the heavy heat. The man stood in the doorway, his eyes caressing her. And with each shift of his gaze, the man hardened as he imagined himself sinking deep into the sleeping beauty's delicious, wet folds.

He went to her, crouching on the bed where she slept, one arm tossed over her face to block the dim light. Gently, he pressed his hands to her thighs, urging her legs apart. She wore no undergarments, and the image of her sex that was revealed to him caused his member to throb.

Bryce drank in the words slowly, fascinated by the writer's languorous pace, his reverence of both the woman's beauty and her sex.

In the story, the narrator dipped his head, pressing his cheek against the soft, hot flesh of his lover's thigh as he laved her sex with his tongue in long, gentle strokes. Beneath his ministrations, the woman squirmed, but didn't awaken.

Her body, though, responded as if she were awake and in his arms. Her nub hardened under his tongue, plumping and throbbing in silent demand for his touch. She writhed beneath his attentions, even in sleep her body seeking that most exquisite of releases.

He kissed her deeply, intimately, his tongue slipping inside to stroke hot, demanding flesh. Small shivers shook the woman's body, building in power until she awoke from the sound of her own voice, crying out her lover's name as wave after wave of orgasmic pleasure crashed over her.

Bryce exhaled, his own body thrumming as if he himself had touched the sleeping woman. He thought of Joan alone in the next room, imagined her laid out on top of the hotel's fine linens. Perhaps asleep, perhaps not. But either way, ready for him.

He smiled, his erection throbbing insistently.

Oh, yes. Joan had given him one hell of a first assignment. And Bryce intended to ace the class.

JOAN SHUT the louvered doors behind her as she entered the bedroom. The bed loomed large, the focal point for the entire room, and Joan was drawn to it.

Four o'clock in the morning, and she wasn't the least bit tired. On the contrary, she'd rarely felt more alive. Her body hummed with a sensual energy and she craved Bryce's hands on her.

She'd tossed her resolution to the wayside...and she couldn't be happier.

Reaching back, she tugged her zipper down, then shimmied out of the dress, leaving it on the floor as if it were one of Hansel and Gretel's breadcrumbs leading the way home. One more step toward the bed and she left her bra. The last step, and she left her garter belt. The thong panties had long been abandoned on the living room floor.

She crawled onto the bed. The spread was some sort of silk or satin, smooth and cool to the touch, a welcome sensation against her burning hot skin. She kept the spread on, peeling it back only to retrieve a pillow.

Her thoughts raced, imagining Bryce's hands on her body, wondering where he was in the story, wondering if he was as turned on by reading it as she hoped. It had been one of her most persistent fantasies ever since she'd read the passage in the Harris book—being awakened by a lover only to realize he'd already started making love to her. His tongue on her most intimate parts. His hands on her breasts. His breath, hot and moist between her legs.

She'd wake up and be consumed by this man, this lover, who would make her come. And then, once she was awake, start all over again, only slowly this time so that she missed none of it.

Joan shivered, hugging the pillow close. It wasn't a fantasy she'd ever shared before. Somehow the moment for sharing just never came up. Now, though, she was glad. She wanted this experience first with Bryce. Stupid, she knew. She was falling for this man—this singular guy who filled every one of her fantasies to a T. She was setting herself up to get hurt, but somehow she just couldn't help it. She wanted him, and, right then, she'd take him however she could get him—and as many times, too.

He'd walk away in the end. A guy like Bryce certainly had no reason to stay. But Joan had nursed a broken heart before, and in the meantime…

Well, in the meantime, she could pretend that he

was Mr. Right. That he could give her a happily ever after.

She snuggled into the pillow, breathing in the fresh scent of the hotel's detergent. Luxury. She closed her eyes. She wanted this fantasy, wanted the whole thing, and that meant she couldn't be awake when Bryce walked through those doors.

If he walked through those doors.

She pressed her lips together, for the first time worrying that Bryce wouldn't be nearly as turned on by his first assignment as she was. But no. She wasn't really worried. She was in tune with this man, and she knew without a doubt that his touch would awaken her.

Assuming, of course, that she could fall asleep in the first place....

She snuggled closer to the pillow and took one last glance at the clock before closing her eyes—3:48. Deep breaths, that was the ticket. And clearing her mind. No thoughts of Bryce. No thoughts of anything. Just drifting.

Her head buzzed, the combination of the wine and the late hour. But then the buzz faded, and there was just the feeling of floating....

OH MY.

Joan's eyes flickered open. Four-fifteen. She'd fallen asleep, and now she was drifting back to consciousness on a blanket of electrical sparks tingling over every inch of her body. She lazily traced her hand up to stroke her erect nipples.

Her thighs were hot, and she could feel the scrape of his beard stubble against the tender skin. *Bryce.* He'd come, just like she'd known he would. Just like in the book.

Just like in her fantasies...

Her sex throbbed with need, and she shifted shamelessly on the bed, wanting him to take her in his mouth, to lave her, and to find and tease that one crucial spot.

His mouth closed over her, the most intimate of kisses, and she lost herself in the hot, wet heat. Her entire body seemed to have folded in on itself, until all that was left was a bundle of sensations craving release. A release that couldn't quite come.

And then, just when she thought he never would, his tongue flicked over her. One stroke, but that was all it took. Joan cried out as she bucked against the bed, unable to control her body and certainly not willing to try. She was simply reacting, not even thinking except for the vaguely muddled thoughts—*yes* and *please* and *don't stop.*

Don't stop.

She must have said the words because Bryce pressed the pad of his thumb against her sex, rubbing in slow, sensuous circles just long enough to speak one simple word. "Never."

Joan smiled, spreading her legs wider as she surrendered to his continued attentions. She'd known it was coming—hell, she'd orchestrated it—but the reality still surprised her. Bryce had made her fantasy come true. And before their confinement was over, Joan intended to return the favor.

BRYCE BURNED WITH NEED. He craved her, wanted to lose himself in her, and desire filled him like a red-hot liquid.

The moment Joan had awakened, trembling, under his touch, Bryce's ability to reason, to think, to do anything other than touch this woman had evaporated like mist. She amused him, intrigued him, fascinated him. But most of all, Joan turned him on like no woman had before.

He didn't know if it was their confinement, the titillating lesson, or simply the woman herself. A woman who knew what she wanted and went after it with a guilelessness and humor that Bryce found refreshing.

The reason didn't matter. Right then, all Bryce wanted was to crawl inside her, to pull her around him and lose himself in her sweetness. He wanted to make love to her until the sun streamed in through the east window, and then he wanted to start all over again.

"Bryce..."

She whispered his name, and her voice cascaded over him. He kissed her intimately, breathing deeply of her sweet, feminine scent. He was as hard as steel, and it was all he could do not to raise himself up and plunge deep inside her.

Not yet…

With the pad of his thumb, he teased her, dipping into her wet heat. His other hand explored her skin, caressing her firm belly, delighting in the way her muscles tensed under his lightest of touches.

He'd been ready the second he'd finished reading the passage, but when he'd stepped into the bedroom, Bryce had come close to losing it. There she was, naked on top of the spread. Her legs were slightly parted, giving him the most enticing view imaginable. She'd either been asleep or faking it, but she'd come alive under his touch, filling him with wave after wave of masculine power.

Now, she murmured his name, her fingers twining in his hair. "Please," she whispered, the word little more than breath.

Bryce wasn't about to quibble. He wanted this woman. Wanted to possess her, to lose himself in her. Her legs shifted, widening in unmistakable invitation. Bryce didn't hesitate. He'd tucked a condom into his pocket before entering the room, and now he sheathed himself, grateful that he'd thought ahead. He didn't want to slow down, didn't want anything that would take him away from this moment.

Slowly, he brushed his lips over the soft skin of her inner thigh, then moved his attention higher. Her hips, her belly. His tongue flicked over her navel, and he watched with supreme satisfaction as her stomach tightened and she trembled beneath his touch. Her fingers still curled in his hair, and she urged him up. He went willingly, one hand resting between her legs as his mouth found her nipple, hard and insistent beneath his tongue.

With the tip of his tongue, he teased her, flicking her nipple and then lowering his mouth to suckle the puckered, rosy flesh. While his mouth focused on her breast, his hand stroked her sex, his fingers dipping inside her soft, wet folds. She rocked her hips, drawing him in deeper and deeper.

He was throbbing, desperate, couldn't stand it anymore. With one bold move he lifted himself up, his arms on either side of her, palms flat against the mattress. She was stunningly beautiful. Pale skin and golden hair accented by enormous blue eyes and full red lips.

The tip of his shaft teased her, the slight contact tormenting both of them.

"Now," she whispered.

He didn't hesitate, and with one quick thrust, he entered her. Her body welcomed him, her slick heat enveloping him like a glove.

He pulled out, then thrust in again, repeating the motion as she lifted her hips, her own rocking motion matching his. She closed her eyes, but Bryce watched, wanting to see every flash of passion, every hint of desire. He wanted her to come in his arms, and he wanted to see the spark in her face when she did.

She made love exuberantly, rising to meet his thrusts, her skin flush with the heat of desire. Her hands curved around his waist and he felt the pinch of her nails in his flesh as she urged him down, harder and deeper.

She whispered his name, then repeated it, again and again. Her voice, deep with passion, seemed to stroke him. He latched on, riding the crest of her voice, each thrust taking him that much closer to release.

"Bryce, please. *Now.*"

Her demand broke over him as he reached the crest, and his entire body seemed to explode, brought to the brink by the thread of pure need running through her voice. Spent, he sagged against her, rolling to one side so as not to crush her under his weight. She murmured, a soft sound of protest, then spooned against him.

He stroked her hair, enjoying the closeness wrought from the circumstances. So often when he was with a woman the first thing on his mind after sex was getting up, getting dressed and getting to the next meeting. Or the gym. Or the office. Or any one of a million little things that made up the ins and outs of his life lately.

Right now, he could do none of that. He and Joan were trapped. And yet he wasn't feeling antsy. Wasn't itching to check his e-mail or call Leo or review a profit-and-loss statement. Instead, he just wanted to hold her. He told himself it was only his unconscious taking advantage of a forced vacation. But he didn't really believe that. No, for the first time in his life, he'd met a woman who interested him more than his work. And that, he thought, said a lot about Joan Benetti.

9

FIVE O'CLOCK IN THE MORNING.

Bleary-eyed, Clive glanced again at the clock on the far side of the kitchen. He'd been up for almost twenty-four hours. His body was humming, and he didn't feel tired, but he knew he had to be. What he thought was crystal-clear thinking was really getting muddled. And soon enough, that would come back to bite him in the ass.

Damn Worthington.

And damn that bitch. The bitch in the purple dress who'd gone and muddled his plans. Worthington's little whore.

Clive had worked the whole scenario out so beautifully, but everything had gone and gotten screwed. And all because of her.

He'd cased the hotel for days. Knew Angela's routine—the private elevator to the penthouse, entering with her passkey, leaving the tray on the coffee table in the empty living room, then leaving. There was nothing—*nothing*—to prevent Clive from simply slipping onto the elevator with Angie and forcing her to let him in that apartment. Or else.

Of course, he'd have kept her up there. Couldn't have her running back down and shooting off her mouth. But he'd planned for that, too. Hell, he'd planned for everything. Everything except a clumsy waiter and a busted duffel bag.

He was seated in a chair, the rifle tight in his hands as he surveyed his seven hostages. They were huddled together in the corner where he'd forced them, a few actually sleeping despite the circumstances. Four were awake, though, staring at him through bloodshot, terrified eyes.

Angie opened her mouth. The only one whose name he knew.

She made a little sound, something like a squeak.

"What?" he demanded, irritation blooming. He didn't need this shit.

Her eyes widened and she shook her head, her lips pressed tight together.

"What?" he repeated, his hand tightening around the gun.

Her gaze dipped to the rifle. "I... Why? Why are y-you doing this?"

He almost didn't answer. Shit, it wasn't any of her business. But people needed to know. Needed to understand what that bastard had done to him.

"He's got to learn," Clive said. "Learn that he can't just play with people's lives. Can't buy out companies and then lay off entire departments. There are *consequences,* you know?"

She nodded, as if she really did understand. How could she? How could anyone? Except maybe Emily. But she was dead now.

His stomach twisted with the memory of his wife.

"Who?" Angie asked. "Who needs to learn?"

He glared at her. He should have known she wouldn't understand. He didn't answer. He just ignored her. She wasn't worth the answer. She'd played a part in messing up his plan, and he sure as hell wasn't going to reward her for that.

No, this was too much. This had never been part of the plan. This wasn't about anybody but Worthington, and now that bitch had gone and turned it into this whole big mess.

He went over his plan in his head again. He had to get out of there. Had to follow the routine as much as he could. He'd rehearsed, dammit, and he was just going to have to buckle down and make this work.

His primary escape route had been from the roof, accessed from the hall outside Worthington's room. No good. Getting back up to the roof was too risky. His secondary escape route was the way to go. And while it had been the trickier route from the penthouse, from the kitchen it was almost easy.

If the primary plan with Worthington had gone awry, then Clive would have led the bastard down the fifteen flights of stairs to the main landing, and then down two more into the sub-basement. From there, they could access the hotel's utility room, where linens were washed and pressed on-site.

His secret passage was behind washer number three.

Clive had done his homework, all right. He doubted even the police knew about his secondary route. He needed to take it. Needed to go now. But the second he stepped away from his seven little sheep, they'd start bleating. He'd have to kill them, and he didn't want to. Killing was only for Worthington. The security guard had been stupid. That hadn't been Clive's fault. The guy had been dumb, and he'd brought it on himself.

But the sheep were cooperating. And Clive wouldn't kill them unless they made him.

He sucked in air, his breath hot and stale through the stocking he still wore over his head. He'd come into the hotel with only one goal—make Worthington pay. A death for a death. Now he'd added another goal. Escaping alive.

The only question was how.

He looked again at Angie, noticing with satisfaction how she drew back, her eyes wide with fear. If he was right, she just might be the solution to his problem.

JOAN AWOKE to find Bryce's hand pressed against her bare hip, creating a warmth that spread throughout her entire body. She sighed, knowing she was grinning like the Cheshire cat, and pressed a soft kiss against his shoulder. This was nice, and despite the horrific circumstances that had brought them together, she really didn't want it to end.

Carefully, so as not to wake him, she slid out from under the covers. She grabbed a plush robe from the back of the bathroom door, then padded into the living area. She didn't want to worry her parents, but neither did she want them to inadvertently discover her predicament. At least she knew they hadn't already heard the news. Her mom had her cell phone number on speed dial and used it liberally in case of mall sales and traffic pileups. The fact that she hadn't heard from her mom made it obvious neither the police nor the media had spilled that she was trapped in the hotel.

She punched in the number and listened to it ring. If she was lucky, she'd catch them before they left for work. She took a deep breath, wondering as she did what the heck she was going to say. *Hi, Mom. I'm in the middle of all this hostage stuff, but don't worry. Donovan told me it's cooled down and I'm safe.* She shrugged. That sounded pretty good.

But when her mom answered, calm and cool and collected flew right out the window. Instead of words, Joan managed one choking sob, then sank to the floor with the phone pressed against her ear.

"Hello? Hello?"

"M-m-mom?" Joan managed to say.

''Joanie? Sweetie, are you all right? Peter, it's Joanie! Something's wrong.''

A rustling noise, and then her father's voice came on the line. ''Jo-jo? What's wrong? Where are you? Are you all right?''

Despite everything, Joan smiled, feeling better already. She took a deep breath. ''I'm—I'm okay. Really.'' Another breath. ''I'm sorry to scare you. I just—''

''What is it? Peter, is Joanie okay? Are you okay?'' Her mom had picked up the extension.

''She's fine, Abby. She was just going to tell me what's wrong.'' Her father's deep soothing voice washed over her. ''What is it, Princess? A fight with a boyfriend?''

At that, Joan had to smile. She'd been a million miles from fighting with Bryce. ''No,'' she said. ''In fact the guy part of the equation is the only good thing about all of this.''

Her parents didn't ask the obvious question—all of what? After twenty-four years, they'd figured out they needed to let her approach difficult topics in her own unique and convoluted way.

''Have you guys been watching the news?''

Her father said no, but her mother drew in a sharp breath. ''Joanie, not the thing at the Monteleone?''

''I'm okay,'' Joan rushed to assure her. ''It's not like I'm a hostage or anything.''

''Hostage?'' her father asked, his voice booming across the line. ''What are you two talking about?''

''It's *okay,* Daddy.'' Joan rushed to reassure her parents. ''Some nutcase took hostages at Talon and I was in the penthouse of the hotel. But I'm fine. Really.''

''Fine?'' her mother repeated. Now Joan could hear the steady buzz of the television in the background. ''My God, Joanie. The news says they've evacuated the hotel.''

''It's okay, Mom. The cops have it all under control. I talked to Donovan and everything. They're wrapping up, doing the negotiating thing with the gunman. It's not dangerous. Just inconvenient.''

''But they *evacuated,*'' her mom repeated. ''Where are you?''

''I'm in the penthouse. They didn't evacuate the penthouse.''

''Well, why on earth not?'' her father said.

Joan shrugged. ''It doesn't matter, Daddy. The point is, I'm safe. I just wanted y'all to know.''

''Is there still room service? What are you going to eat? They can't make you starve.''

''It's *fine,* Mom. The penthouse has a kitchen.'' She didn't mention that it was essentially bare.

''I'll make some calls,'' her dad said in his familiar no-nonsense voice.

Joan smiled. Peter Benetti worked on an assembly line at Gribell Helicopter, on his feet all day doing backbreaking work. Which meant that at night he sat down at Pritchard's, a popular Trenton hangout for both the Gribell workers and the Jersey cops.

"Listen," Joan said, "I should go. I don't have my cell phone charger and the land lines are down. So I want to save the battery. I just wanted you to know."

She caught a movement out of the corner of her eye and looked up to see Bryce lounging in the doorway to the bedroom, watching her with curious eyes.

"You call us if you need anything," her mom said.

"Are you alone?" her dad said.

"No, Daddy. I was, um, delivering some books for the store when it happened." She met Bryce's eyes, saw that the curious expression had been replaced by one of amusement. "He's been very nice about sharing his space with me."

"Dinner," her mother said. "My meat loaf."

Joan blinked. "Pardon me?"

"Friday," her mom said firmly, as if saying it would ensure that the crisis would be over. "Yes. Come over Friday night and bring the young man with you."

"Um, Mom, that's very nice, but he might have other plans."

"What's that?" Bryce said, loud enough for her parents to hear. He moved to her side, sliding his fingertips under the collar of the thick terry cloth robe.

"Is that him?" her mom said. "You tell him we insist."

Bryce's fingers stroked her collarbone, and Joan shivered, his touch sparking a million tiny goose bumps. At the same time, she glared at him. She could hardly fabricate a lie now that her parents had overheard the question.

"My mother wants you to come for dinner Friday," she said, the words emerging on a shaky breath. "A thank-you, I guess, for being so hospitable. You don't have to feel obligated."

"Nonsense," Bryce said. "I'd be delighted."

"Great," Joan said, not entirely certain it *was* great. She didn't want illusions about this man. Didn't want to believe that what they shared inside the penthouse could translate to the real world. They were in fantasy land right now, some magic netherworld. But past that door...that was reality. And Joan's reality didn't mesh with Bryce's. She knew that; she just didn't want to think about it.

"Friday," her mother said firmly.

Joan drew in a breath and nodded, realizing this was her mother's way of making the abnormal seem normal. "Absolutely, Mom. Friday."

AS JOAN FLIPPED HER phone closed, Bryce wondered what he'd just agreed to—and why. No, that wasn't true. He knew why. He wanted an excuse to see Joan again, even after this crisis was over.

Even that, though, wasn't entirely true. With any other woman, he would have simply pulled out his day planner and made arrangements for dinner or drinks. With Joan, he'd gravitated toward meeting her parents.

For the bulk of his adult life, he'd avoided getting close to women. He'd seen how a trusting relationship had devastated his father. Hell, it had devastated Bryce, too. Why put himself through that? It wasn't as if his life was empty. His work filled it to overflowing. In fact, he didn't have time for a relationship even if he wanted one. Which he didn't.

And yet he was having dinner with Joan's parents.

He frowned, not liking the implications.

With effort, he shook off the contemplative mood. There was no unconscious motive. Rather, the opportunity had arisen, and he'd taken it. That was, after all, what he did best. No sense second-guessing himself now.

He realized that Joan was staring at him, her lips slightly parted, her brow furrowed.

"I think there's some coffee in here," he said, brushing past her.

She followed. "Do you realize you're stuck now? My mom will have a fit if you *don't* come to dinner."

"I'm looking forward to it," he said. And he was. Despite the implications, despite the feeling that this woman could make him lose control in more than just the bedroom.

Joan pushed past him, then bent down to look in the cupboards. "You're right," she said. "There's coffee.'' She opened the tiny refrigerator. ''No cream, though. Do you take it black?''

''I can handle it.''

She nodded, then started a pot of coffee. ''There's orange juice, too,'' she said. ''And you mentioned vodka.''

He laughed. ''Coffee and screwdrivers. Hell of a breakfast.''

She grinned, a little sheepish. ''Believe it or not, breakfast is the one meal I can cook. I make fabulous waffles, and my omelettes are to die for. But you haven't exactly left me a whole lot to work with here.''

She propped a fist on her hip and stared at him, silently challenging him to insult her culinary skills. Bryce laughed, then tugged her close, planting a quick kiss on her cheek, then sliding down to meet her mouth. She made a startled little noise, then matched his kiss with an enthusiasm that made him wonder if they shouldn't forget breakfast altogether and head straight back into the bedroom.

When she pulled away, her face wore a lopsided grin. ''No way, mister,'' she said. ''You owe me some tat.''

''That I do,'' he said. ''How about business over breakfast?''

She nodded. ''Good.'' She poured them both a glass of orange juice, then looked at him. ''Vodka?''

Bryce shook his head. He never drank in the morning. "Help yourself, though."

"No way," she said. "Considering everything, I think I want to keep a clear head." She ran her teeth over her lower lip, her brow furrowing with worry. "My mom's right, you know. We're going to get hungry if they don't let us out of here soon."

"I'm sure they will," he said. Bryce couldn't imagine this dragging on much longer. "Which means we better get started with your tat." He checked his watch. "And now's as good a time as any."

He headed back into the bedroom, gesturing for her to follow. She did, but her expression was dubious, becoming even more so when he climbed onto the bed and patted the mattress beside him.

"*My* turn, remember? Business, not bed."

"Trust me."

Joan didn't look convinced, but she climbed into bed and settled back, a pile of pillows plumped up behind her.

He punched the remote, turning the television on. They checked out the news first, learning nothing they didn't already know about the situation downstairs. While Joan had been speaking to her parents, Gordon had called Bryce back. No news there, and so Bryce had next called Leo. But all the attorney had to report was that he was providing the police with Bryce's crank file—the file with all the threatening letters

Bryce had received over the last ten years. Bryce wasn't surprised. He was savvy enough to know that this situation may be centered around him.

He hated the possibility. Hated the fact that some madman was threatening innocent people because of him. And hated it even more because he'd spent so much of his career trying to make sure as few people as possible got injured as a result of his deals. He shook his head. Some irony.

"Bryce?" Joan's brow furrowed.

"I'm fine," he said, then tuned into the financial channel. With effort, he forced his mind back to the present. "Lesson number one," he said, using the remote to gesture toward the screen. "In the business world, you need to keep up with your competition and keep an eye open for opportunities."

"Right," she said. "Competition and opportunities. Got it."

He settled in, hooking an arm around her shoulder. She snuggled close, and, despite the short amount of sleep they'd gotten, she stayed awake for the entire two hours that he watched the program. Not only did she stay awake, she even asked some questions—damned insightful ones, too—when the commentator started discussing Warren Buffett's investment strategies and successes.

As soon as the show was over, Bryce clicked the television off and turned to her. "Have you watched this show before?"

Her brows lifted. "Oh, sure. All the time. I never miss it." She frowned, then shook her head. "Okay, that was a big fat lie. I never miss *The Simpsons,* and I was totally addicted to *Survivor.* But this stuff...no way."

He laughed. "I suppose if we had a camera in here, this would almost be like a *Survivor* episode."

She scooted around and kneeled on the bed in front of him, the robe tucked under her knees. "Sort of," she said. "Especially if we end up stuck in here and have to eat bugs."

"The hotel management will have a fit if they hear you suggesting there are bugs in this suite."

She just grinned. "Probably. At any rate, it's not really *Survivor* material. I'd say it's more *Big Brother* meets *Joe Millionaire.*"

Bryce shook his head, not familiar with the program.

"They sent all these women to live with this guy in a castle, and told them he was a millionaire. But he wasn't really. And each girl wanted him to fall in love with her, and then he picked one girl and had to tell her that he wasn't really rich."

"How'd she react?" Bryce could guess. In his experience, he hadn't met a woman yet who he believed would stay with him if he wasn't rich. Although maybe Joan...

He shook his head, not interested in letting his thoughts go that way.

''She stayed,'' Joan said.

''Are they still together?''

She blushed. ''I don't know,'' she admitted. ''I was mostly just interested in the fairy-tale part.'' She licked her lips and looked him in the eyes. ''I like to believe in happily ever after.''

She looked so innocent that he kissed the tip of her nose. ''We all do.''

The blush deepened, and she shook her head. He had the feeling she'd said more than she planned, and he smiled to himself, pleased that, subconsciously she trusted him enough to drop her guard for a moment.

''Actually,'' she continued, ''I only watched a few episodes and missed the finale altogether. But it was all over the news. I'm surprised you missed it.''

''The financial news has a remarkably limited scope,'' he said.

''You need to broaden your horizons.''

''I thought that was what I was doing with you.''

She tapped the side of her nose. ''Righto.''

''So why'd you only watch a few episodes of the millionaire show?''

She shrugged. ''I guess I liked the concept better than the execution.''

A knot of disappointment settled in Bryce's gut. ''The idea of marrying a millionaire?''

''No,'' Joan said. ''I mean, that would be awesome, of course, but—'' She cut herself off, then stared at him, her cheeks blooming pink. Apparently, she'd just remembered the bulk of his bank account. "Well, it *would* be cool," she said defensively. "But what I liked was the idea of pretending to be someone you're not."

"Really?" Bryce's pulse increased as he remembered her fib about her academic achievements. Did she actually have a motive that made sense? "Who do you want to be?"

"Oh, no one, I guess. I mean, I don't have some big fantasy life in mind. I just thought the concept was neat."

"You're happy with your life," Bryce said. It was a statement, not a question.

"Yeah, I guess I am. I love my job. My parents are great. I don't have a steady boyfriend, but I've got time before I need to get all weirded out by the biological clock thing." She shrugged. "Overall, I'd say things are going pretty well." Her brow furrowed with her frown. "I mean, assuming we don't have to stay in this penthouse for the rest of our natural lives."

Bryce just shook his head.

"What?"

"I so rarely meet people who admit to being happy with their lives." As he spoke the words, he realized how true it was. Most everyone he knew wanted what was over the horizon, beyond the next conquest. They were never happy with the here and now. Himself included. He'd never thought of that as a character flaw, but now he wondered what he was trying to prove. Was it really his personality to be so driven, or was he running from something? From women like Joan who could make him slow down and watch the world as it went by?

"Happy, yes," Joan said with a laugh. "I'm also as flighty as they come." She slid off the bed and padded into the other room. "Orange juice?" she called over her shoulder.

"Sure."

She came back with the carton of orange juice, then refilled their glasses.

She handed him the glass, then took a sip of hers, regarding him over the rim. "Actually, I owe you an apology."

"The Ph.D.?" he blurted out, then cringed. It had become desperately important to him that she admit the fib.

Her eyes widened. "How'd you know?"

"I'm a brilliant businessman, remember? And you're probably a lousy poker player."

She spread her hands out in a gesture of supplication. "So you caught me. You've had erotica lessons from a fraud."

"Now *that,*" he said, "is not true." He straightened his leg, until his foot pressed against her thigh. "You definitely know your stuff."

"Good. Then I didn't void our deal."

"Not at all." He let his gaze skim over her. She

looked so innocent sitting there in a fluffy white bathrobe. But he knew better. The woman under that terry cloth was a long way from innocent. And that was good news for him.

"I'm looking forward to my next lesson," he said. "But why did you tell me all that stuff about having the Ph.D.?"

"Oh," she said, "that's easy. I'd already lied to you about co-owning the store, so—"

"Wait," he said, holding up a hand. That lie he hadn't caught. "Why did you lie about that?"

Her gaze wavered and she looked a little sheepish. "That dress-for-success thing," she said.

Bryce shook his head, not following.

"Ronnie's thinking about cutting the store's hours or finding a partner. And, well, I want to convince her to bring me in as an owner. And all those books say that you should act like you already have the job you want, so—"

"So you figured you needed those kind of credentials."

"Yeah," she agreed. "Well, that and I, uh, wanted you to take me up on the trade. I didn't know if you'd be interested in trading business for erotica with a bookstore clerk."

"Makes sense," he said, relieved that it did, in fact, make sense. "So were you more interested in learning about business, or sharing erotic knowledge?"

She licked her lips. ‘‘Both held a certain appeal. But…’’

She trailed off, and Bryce couldn’t help but laugh. ‘‘I get it,’’ he said. ‘‘You came up here with an agenda.’’

Her shoulders sagged. ‘‘Guilty.’’

‘‘Well, I’m happy to fulfill my end of the bargain, but if Ronnie’s interested in bringing in as a partner, she probably needs someone who can bring cash to the deal.’’

Joan nodded, her mouth curving down into a frown. ‘‘I know. That was another reason I wanted to come up here. You said you’d buy three first editions, remember?’’ She knit her fingers together. ‘‘Um, are you still going to buy them?’’

Bryce laughed. ‘‘There’s definitely nothing wrong with your salesmanship abilities.’’

Her cheeks colored. ‘‘Sorry. It’s just that the store’s had a terrible year so far, and I figured that if I brought in some serious money, then Ronnie would maybe let me work full-time even if she doesn’t want me as a partner.’’

‘‘Serious money, huh?’’

‘‘Well, they *are* first editions…’’

‘‘I see.’’ He put on his negotiator’s face. ‘‘I didn’t get where I am by wasting money.’’

She raised an eyebrow, then sat up straighter. ‘‘I bet you didn’t get where you are by welshing on deals, either. You said three, and I don't recall being handed a budget."

Bryce laughed, then leaned forward to kiss her.

Her eyes widened. "What was that for?"

He had no idea. The woman simply charmed him. "I'll buy the books," he said. "Don't worry."

"Good." She nodded, clearly relieved. "So what else? Teach me everything. My own little miniature MBA."

He nodded toward the television. "That was lesson number one. Not as scintillating as *Survivor,* but did you manage to stay awake?"

She cocked an eyebrow, indignant. "Awake? I thought it was interesting." She ran her fingers through her hair, pushing the loose curls off her forehead as she shifted on the bed. She ended up sitting cross-legged in front of him, her face animated, the robe tucked modestly around her. "I mean, I never thought to watch it before, but it was kind of cool. And I liked that quote from the Margaritaville guy."

He held up a hand. "*Warren* Buffett. Not Jimmy."

She rolled her eyes. "You knew who I meant. My point is it made a lot of sense. Price is what you pay and value is what you get, or something like that."

"Pop quiz. Apply it to your business."

She grinned, and he knew she'd seen that one coming. "Like buying a first edition at an estate sale for twenty bucks when it's worth four hundred. The idea is to keep the price down and the value up."

He tapped her on the nose. "If you're not careful, you're going to turn into the teacher's pet."

"Yeah?" She uncrossed her legs, sliding her foot out and then stroking his thigh with her toes. "I can live with that."

He closed his eyes, letting the heat generated by her touch wash over him.

"So tell me more," she said, her voice low with a teasing edge.

"You're trying to distract me," he said.

"Me? Never."

"Hmm. I think a little game is in order for lesson number two."

She pulled her foot away, then rested her chin on her knee. "What kind of game?"

He nodded to the armoire. "Top shelf. Under the spare blanket."

She got up, moving to the armoire. After pulling the blanket off, she turned to him with a grin. "Monopoly?"

"Not just Monopoly, sweetheart. Strip Monopoly. Think you can handle it?"

She laughed, the sound delighting him.

"Oh yeah," she said. "I think I can handle that just fine."

10

HE WAS REAMING HER in Monopoly. He owned Park Place and almost everything else, and all she owned was Baltic Avenue. Not only that, but she was paying rent on his hotels out the wazoo, and she kept ending up in jail.

Needless to say, she was pretty nearly naked.

Being a gentleman, Bryce had lent her a pair of boxers, some sweatpants and a T-shirt. She'd helped herself to a pair of socks and put her bra back on. Then she'd slipped the bathrobe on over the entire thing.

He'd started out in nothing more than gray sweats and a T-shirt. No socks and, she was pretty sure, no underwear.

Even so, he remained fully dressed.

She was sitting there with only his boxer shorts for modesty. "This isn't fair, you know," she said.

His gaze drifted to her breasts, her traitorous nipples peaking under the scrutiny. "Maybe not," he said. "But it's a hell of a lot of fun."

She scowled, rolled the die, and ended up on one

of his railroads. He owned them all, so they were hard to avoid. She sighed. "How much?"

He glanced at the tiny pile of bills by her knee. "You don't have enough." He waggled his fingers in her general direction. "Okay. Drop them."

"Argh!" She flopped back on the bed. "No fair." She rolled around, ending up on her stomach with her feet in the air. She gathered the covers up under her chest, reducing her bareness, which increased her ability to concentrate exponentially. "I'm not dropping anything until you drop some more information."

A slow smile spread across his face. The smile of a supremely confident man. "Mutiny," he said.

"Maybe." She nodded toward the board. "Come on. Information. Give."

"Fair enough." He shifted, stretching his legs out parallel to hers.

They weren't touching at all, and yet she could feel him. His presence alone turned her on more than she could have ever imagined.

"You've learned a lot about business in the last forty minutes," he said, his tone managing to be both playful and serious. "I'm sure of it." He plucked a hotel off a property and held it up for her. "For example, tell me about this."

"Real estate," she said. "Just like in Manhattan, I'm getting screwed on rent."

His gaze ran the length of her near-naked form.

"But I'm making out like a bandit," he said. He rolled onto his back, his hands intertwined behind his head. "That's how I got started, you know."

"Hotels?"

"Real estate." He turned his head, meeting her eyes. "Construction, actually. I started at the bottom."

"Sort of like where I am now," she said. "In real life and Monopoly."

"Something like that."

"So how'd you get into it?" she asked.

He reached out, running his fingers under the waistband of the boxers she was wearing. "If I tell you, will you take those off? I won fair and square. I want my prize."

She lifted her chin. "Tell me. Then we'll talk."

He made a low growling noise, and she laughed, moving away as he lunged across the bed toward her.

"Missed me!"

"I won't miss again," he said.

"I hope not." She met his gaze, enjoying the way his eyes flashed with need. "Now tell."

"I was working your basic construction gigs. Just a kid," he said after a brief pause. "And then I bought a building and fixed it up. And while I was doing that, I learned a bit about repairs and renovations. Then I sold the property and learned something about real estate." He shrugged. "It just sort of snowballed from there."

"Wow," she said. "I'm impressed."

"Thanks."

She scooted forward, then ran the palm of her hand over the tips of his fingers. "That explains it."

"Explains what?"

"Your hands are rough."

"Too rough?" he asked, his voice low and intimate.

She shook her head, a tingle shooting up her spine merely from the sound of his voice. "Not at all," she said. "Perfect." She frowned. "But you don't work in construction…"

"That was more than ten years ago," he said. "I work at a desk now."

"Oh." Her brow furrowed. "You must have one hell of a rough typewriter."

"Habitat for Humanity," he said. "Keeps my hand in construction, gets me out of the office, and it's a good cause."

"You miss it," she said. "The hands-on stuff, I mean."

He nodded, silent, and she saw something flash in his eyes. Regret, maybe?

"I always thought I'd like to do something like that," Joan continued. "Like Habitat. But I can barely tell a hammer from a screwdriver."

"If you're interested, you should go anyway. They can find work for pretty much every skill level. Besides," he added, "you seem like a quick learner."

"I am," she said.

"That's my business advice for you," he said.

Her brow creased. "Habitat for Humanity?"

"Being a quick study. Pay attention to things. Learn by doing."

"Hmmm," she said. "That much I figured out on my own."

"You've already taught yourself about the erotica. What else have you studied?"

"Rare books in general," she said. "And marketing. I read a whole bunch on that and then I called and talked to the owners of some other bookstores in town."

"Good. Cooperative marketing, being aware of the competition. Important stuff."

"It's the bookkeeping stuff that gets me." The thought of all those numbers made her head spin.

"Me, too," Bryce said. He grinned. "I hire someone to do the numbers part."

"Really? You don't know how to keep books?"

"I know the theory, but I've never put it to practice. The point is to bring the money in. I don't necessarily need to be the person to tally it up. I just need to trust the person I hire to do that for me." He grinned. "You want confirmation that you've got more money coming in than going out."

"*That* I knew."

He rolled onto his side, traced a lazy finger over her thigh. "My point is that you're doing everything right. Make sure Ronnie knows everything you've learned. You're an asset, Joan. I can't imagine she doesn't realize that."

"Thanks," Joan said, trying to focus despite the heat building from his touch. "I really appreciate that." She eyed the board, then sighed. "You really creamed me, you know."

"Absolutely," he said, looking more than a little smug. "Off with your pants."

Joan laughed, then reached across the bed for a pillow and whacked him with it.

"Hey!" He crossed his arms over his face in self-defense. "I won fair and square."

"Oh yeah?" Laughing, she wonked him again. "If you want your reward, you're just going to have to come and take it."

"You drive a hard bargain, babe, but I think I can handle that." As he spoke, he crawled toward her. She started to scramble away—not trying *too* hard—and he caught her around the waist, pulling her back on top of him.

Laughing, Joan wriggled and kicked, her legs in the air above them.

His arm encircled her waist and his free hand slipped under the waistband, tugging the boxers down. Joan squealed and wriggled some more, her wriggling actually helping Bryce in his quest to de-frock her. She stifled a grin. *Oh, darn.*

When the boxers were down around her knees, he

flipped her over, his arms on either side of her head as his knees hugged her hips. Joan quit laughing, her body on fire, as she saw the hunger reflected in his eyes. "Bryce," she whispered.

He lowered his lips to hers, the anticipation almost as sweet as the kiss. It started out slow, almost tentative, but soon his mouth consumed her, as if he had to have her, as if he couldn't have enough.

She opened her mouth to his, exploring and tasting and teasing. Her hands stroked his back. She could feel that his skin was hot, burning, even through the thin material of his T-shirt.

"Take it off," she murmured.

He ignored the request, instead slipping his hand between her legs, finding her already wet. She groaned, her back arching with need, as if trying to draw him in. She needed him inside her, needed to touch him, just needed *him.* And she pulled at his shirt insistently, sliding her hands under and then tugging it up and over his head.

"Joan." Her name was a demand on his lips, and she raised her hips as he tugged the boxers the rest of the way off. Her fingers fumbled for the string to his pants, and he struggled out of them. Before she could even make the demand, he slipped on a condom.

"Now," she demanded. He didn't waste time, thrusting inside her with a need that matched her own. She was so close, so ready, and the orgasm hit almost immediately, forcing her over the edge as she clung to Bryce and forced him along with her.

She breathed deep, unable to remember ever feeling quite so alive. Her body still tingled from wave after glorious wave of pleasure, and still she craved him. And it wasn't even sex she craved. It was everything. Sex and laughter and, most of all, Bryce.

He held her close, and Joan sighed, breathing in his scent.

"It's like those magic doors," she said. "And I don't know that I ever want to open it again."

He shifted to meet her eyes, his expression a question mark.

She shrugged, feeling a little silly. "You know. Like when you're a kid and you read a book and the characters go through a magic door. And they have a fabulous adventure and then, when they come back, it's like they never left their old world." She licked her lips. "I guess I'm not looking forward to going back through that magic door to the real world."

He didn't answer, at least not out loud. Instead, he cupped her cheek in the palm of his hand, stroking her skin as he looked in her eyes. After a moment, he bent and kissed the tip of her nose.

"I'm being silly, aren't I?"

"To the contrary. I think that's one of the nicest compliments a woman has ever paid me."

She smiled, snuggling up close again. "Just so you

know, I really liked my lesson, even if you did literally beat the pants off me.''

''I'm glad,'' he said. ''And just so *you* know. Right now, you're at the head of the class.''

BRYCE HAD THOUGHT Joan would be a distraction. That her constant presence would make it hard for him to manage to get any work done. In fact, he managed almost a full day of work. Quite remarkable considering the circumstances.

And it was even Joan who'd suggested he get his butt out of bed and in gear. ''Can't you work with a phone?'' she'd asked. ''I'm not going to be the cause of you being a slacker.''

He'd laughed, but he'd appreciated her efforts. So many women he dated seemed offended if he even checked his messages in the evening. Joan seemed to realize instinctively that his work was all-encompassing. That it was part of who he was and that sex with Joan would be all the sweeter if it was a reward for a hard day's work.

And so he worked. He got on his cell phone with Leo and managed to straighten out a few issues with the New Jersey deal. He had his New Mexico attorney fax him the specs on a building he was considering buying in Albuquerque, and he reviewed a press release issued by the Carpenter Shipping shareholders objecting to his plans to purchase the company.

Joan even helped, reading the Albuquerque materials and marking in the margin anything she thought sounded odd or interesting about the building. "I like it," had been her ultimate verdict. "It has a history and yet it seems to be in pretty good shape."

"Price to value?"

"Absolutely," she'd replied. "Tons of value." She winked. "And a really nice swimming pool, too."

She'd left him the papers and had disappeared into the bedroom to watch television. For a while, he'd heard the familiar snappy music of *The Simpsons* theme song, and he realized she must have found a rerun. A few other sitcoms followed, and Bryce tuned it out. After a while, he realized he was squinting as he reviewed the papers spread out next to him on the couch. The sun was fast setting, and he'd left Joan all alone for hours.

With a frown, he got up. That hadn't been his intention. He'd appreciated her letting him work, but she was stuck against her will and he hadn't planned to abandon her.

Now he headed into the bedroom, an apology on his lips. When he saw her, though, he stifled the apology and simply grinned.

She was sitting cross-legged on top of the covers, a carton of orange juice on the nightstand and an open jar of olives in her hand. The television was turned on, and instead of the sitcoms he'd tuned out, he now recognized the evening business report. He lifted an eyebrow in question.

"Gotta stay on top of the market," she said. She held out the jar of olives to him. "Dinner?"

Bryce laughed. "Sure." He moved toward her. "Dinner sounds great. And so," he added, "does dessert."

FROM THE LOOK in his eye, there was no doubt as to the type of dessert Bryce craved, and Joan allowed herself a satisfied little smile. She'd told herself over and over that she needed to be rational about this. To keep in the forefront of her mind that it was only about sex and business. Tit for tat, and a good time, too. But nothing more.

She had no delusions that anything permanent could develop between her and Bryce.

Yes, that's what she kept telling herself, but it was a lie that was getting harder and harder to sustain.

When she'd first arrived, she'd entertained the fantasy, of course. What woman wouldn't? Trapped for days with a gorgeous, sexy billionaire. But it had been pure fantasy. Bryce wasn't in her league. He lived in a different world, celebrities and corporate bigwigs, and folks who lived in mansions with private jets at their disposal.

Not her world, and she hadn't had any illusions that she could somehow make the leap from her world to his.

Now, though…

Now the man didn't seem quite so mysterious.

He'd started out a lot like her. Just a working-class guy with an urge to do something he enjoyed. And that made Bryce a lot more accessible.

And it made the way she was starting to feel about him a lot more scary.

He was curled up beside her on the bed, and now he touched her cheek. "Penny for your thoughts."

She smiled brightly, realizing where her thoughts had headed, and really not wanting to go there. "Oh, come on. Only a penny? I think you can afford more than that."

"I can afford a lot more," he said, trailing his finger down her cheek, her neck.

Joan trembled, closing her eyes as he caressed her skin, his fingers traveling downward. His hand, rough and strong, slid inside the robe, then cupped her breast. He stroked her nipple, the touch featherlight, and Joan gasped for breath.

"So what's my next lesson?" he asked, his voice low and seductive. "I think it's my turn again."

Joan fought to concentrate, a losing battle considering the way her body was tingling from his touch. She had the perfect lesson in mind for Bryce, but it meant that she had to pull herself together and take charge of the situation. Not an easy task when all she wanted to do was melt in his arms.

"Lessons, Joan." His voice was teasing, as if he entirely understood why she didn't answer. He brushed his lips against her ear, his breath tickling her in a most delicious way. "Is it time for my next lesson?"

A shiver raced up her spine and her mouth went dry. "Actually," she managed, "it is." She pressed the palms of her hands flat against his chest and urged him back. She followed the motion, so that she ended up almost straddling him. "In fact, I've got the perfect lesson for a man like you."

His eyes narrowed just slightly. "A man like me, huh?"

"Yup." She straightened, so that she was now sitting up, her knees on either side of his hips, and her crotch pressed against his waist, just at the band of his sweatpants. The position turned him on—she could tell by the press of his erection against her rear—and she enjoyed the little surge of power. At the moment, she was in control, and she intended to stay that way.

"What kind of man is that?"

She just smiled, then leaned over him to the bedside table where the copy of *Pleasures* sat, a piece of paper marking the passage she'd assigned Bryce to read earlier. She picked up the book, then flipped pages. Then she found it. A section that had always enticed, always stirred up delightful, decadent fantasies. Fantasies she wanted to play out with this man.

"Here," she said, pointing. She watched as he read. He kept his face impassive, but his eyes gave him away. There was interest there, and she knew that, even without him saying a word, he understood exactly what she wanted. She allowed herself a tiny grin. "Today's lesson plan," she said.

"I think I like this school."

She raised an eyebrow as she pulled the cloth tie free from her robe. Then she tugged his hands forward, and bound his wrists with the sash. As she did so, the tempo of her pulse increased, and she saw that his breathing had sped up, too. He was intrigued, turned on. And she loved the power of knowing that she was the one making him hot.

When his wrists were bound with one end of the sash and she held the other in her hand, she scooted off of him, shifting her weight until she was standing on the floor. She urged him up into a sitting position.

"You asked me what kind of man," she said. "Can you guess from what you read?"

"You tell me."

"Dominant, of course. In control. Always in charge." She bent down and kissed him hard on the lips, pulling away before his mouth could claim hers. Then she gave the sash a little tug. "Come on, Mr. Worthington," she said. "This lesson is all about submission."

11

BRYCE PULLED at the sash that bound his hands together, but he couldn't move his arms any more than a few inches. Joan had managed to secure his hands tightly to the bed's ornate headboard. The lack of control put him on edge, making the adrenaline pump through his body with even more force than usual when Joan was near.

The passage he'd read had fueled his senses, the words all the more intriguing since he knew that Joan had picked them out with purpose. He could only assume they were words she'd read over and over. Words that turned her on. Words she wanted to act out.

And she'd chosen him to do it with.

That thought alone made him hotter than he'd ever been in his life, and now his body was on alert, primed and ready.

"Trust," she said. "Trust and power. Both of these play into the erotic. Enticing, stimulating…"

"Stimulating," he repeated. Yes, indeed, he was being stimulated, all right.

"Watch me," she whispered.

She crossed to the armoire and pulled out the bottom drawer, finding two candles that the hotel kept in case of a blackout. Just as the woman in the story had done, Joan lit them, propping one on each side of the room. Then she clicked the light switch. Darkness shrouded the room, and then as his eyes adjusted, a warm glow filled the area.

Joan moved to the side of the bed, slipping the robe off as she walked. It fell to the floor a few feet away, and she stood there, naked and beautiful. Were his hands not tied, he could have touched her, caressed her breasts, cupped her sex. He tugged at the bonds, the reaction almost instinctual.

A knowing smile touched her lips. ''Soon,'' she whispered. Her teeth grazed her lower lip. ''Do you remember how this started?'' she asked. ''Us, I mean. In this suite.''

She could mean so many things by that, but he knew exactly what she was talking about—she'd watched him. She'd hidden behind the screen and watched him read the book. He stiffened in anticipation. Was it his turn, he wondered, to be the watcher? If so, then Joan was planning to take this encounter beyond the passage in the book, and somehow that made it all the more seductive. She'd left her comfort zone, left the fantasy of someone else's story. And now she was here, alone, with him.

Her gaze swept over his body, stopping at his

groin. Her lips curled into a satisfied smile and she closed her eyes. "Watch," she said.

She swayed to a music that only she heard, her hips undulating in an erotic motion. *Touch me, want me, come to me.* She didn't speak a word, but he knew what she wanted. Knew all her secret, silent desires. She arched her neck, her fingertips trailing down her neck to the swell of her breasts. Bryce watched, his mouth suddenly parched, as her nipples hardened, the areola dark and puckered.

With both hands, she massaged her breasts. Her eyes were closed, her head thrown back, but even so, somehow Bryce knew that all of her concentration was on him. That he was her focus. That this was for him.

He realized that he'd yanked against the bonds once more. With a mild curse, he fell back against the bed, defeated yet aroused.

She opened her eyes just long enough to smile at him, then her hand trailed down over her belly. Then lower and lower still until her fingers grazed the golden curls between her thighs. Bryce groaned, his entire body ready to explode.

"Joan," he whispered. "You're killing me."

Her smile offered promises of things to come, but no end to the sweet torture of the moment. Not yet. And when her fingers dipped down, exploring her sweet, wet folds, Bryce knew that he was a lost man.

"Do you like that?" he asked.

"Mmmm," she murmured. "I'm pretending it's you. You touching me. Your hand stroking me. Your fingers teasing me." Her breasts rose and fell as her breath came faster and faster. "You inside me."

His body pulsed, imagining the same. Losing himself in her heat, burying himself in her sweetness. "Joan." The name was a plea.

A sultry smile touched her lips and she came to the bed, climbing to kneel beside him. Her fingers reached for the knot of his pants, quickly unfastening the garment. She tugged down the pants, and he lifted his hips, eager to help.

When he was naked, she straddled him, then bent forward at the waist to brush a kiss over his lips. "What do you want?" she whispered, pulling back just far enough to look him in the eyes.

"To touch you," he said. At the moment, Bryce was certain that was all he'd *ever* wanted.

She shook her head, and her defiance turned him on even more. "My rules," she said. "My touch. Although…"

She grabbed the headboard and gave him a seductive smile as she scooted up, lowering herself over his mouth, following the script laid out in *Pleasures.* Letting the text drive their own private pleasures.

He groaned, a desperate low sound, as he arched up, feasting on her sweetness. She wriggled and squirmed, a steady stream of "oh, yes, please" caressing his ears and shooting straight to his groin.

His entire body throbbed and he wasn't at all certain he could survive. He needed to sink inside her. Right then. It seemed imperative. As if he'd go crazy if he couldn't have her, couldn't feel her tighten around him as she lost herself to pleasure.

She knew what he needed, and she slipped back down his body, moving with the sureness of a woman in control. He had no idea when she'd grabbed the condom, but suddenly she was sheathing him, stroking him. She lifted herself up, then settled on him, lowering herself just enough to take the tip of his length inside her.

Bryce groaned, a cry of both pleasure and frustration. His fingers itched to take her, to grasp her hips and thrust her home. He couldn't. Could do nothing but dig his fingernails into his palms as every sensation in his body rushed to his cock.

She thrust down, taking him all the way in, and Bryce lifted his hips to meet her movement. Without the distraction of other touches, other caresses, his entire being centered on their union. He felt her fully, intimately. The sensation was raw, primal and absolutely erotic. It was also overwhelming, and he thrust upwards, deeper and harder, wanting to both consume her and be consumed.

Again and again, closer and closer, until finally his entire body seemed to explode in a massive firestorm. His body trembled, his breath uneven.

He moaned, losing himself to the onslaught of pleasure. And when the waves had subsided, he opened his eyes to see Joan smiling at him, clearly pleased with herself.

"So tell me, sir," she said. "Did you like that?"

"What do you think?"

She ran her hands up his bare chest, then melded her body to his before brushing a kiss over his lips. "I think yes."

"I think you're very perceptive."

"Good." She rolled off him, but pressed close to his side. "I want to be unforgettable," she said.

He stroked her hair, his heart twisting a little. She was unforgettable, all right. And he'd surrendered to her desires so easily, knowing that it felt so right. He'd do it again, too, without the slightest hesitation.

But that was all sex and passion. The part that really made him sweat, that made him tremble with unfamiliar fear, was that tiny, hidden part of himself that knew he would surrender to the woman herself. That maybe, without knowing it, he already had.

And that, of course, was the most unsettling thing of all.

HE FOUND THE TWINE in a cabinet, and now he wound it round and round, binding her wrists. He had to be sure she couldn't get free. Had to make sure he was in control.

On her knees in front of him, Angie grimaced, her eyes bloodshot, her chin quivering. She was holding back tears, and Clive looked away, unwilling to meet her eyes. He didn't want to pity her. Hell, he didn't want to even think about her. He needed her, and that was it. Everything he was doing, he was doing out of necessity. They needed to understand that.

In front of him, the remaining six huddled together. The overhead light was off, but streaks of early morning sunlight crept in through cracks in the closed shutters, casting the hostages in shadow and light. They looked at him, their faces a mix of fear and relief. Fear of him. Relief that it was Angie and not them.

Scum. They deserved this. Being trapped in this room with him, with his gun. If they could so easily toss Angie to the wolf, then they deserved it. *He* was only trying to survive. They'd turned their backs on a friend.

He jerked the cord that bound her wrists, pulling her up to her feet. She stumbled, but didn't fall. She kept her gaze down, not looking at him as he urged her to his side.

He kept the rifle balanced across his legs, then cocked the handgun. One by one, he aimed it at each of the six, making sure he got each forehead in the sights. He wanted them to know—wanted to be sure they understood—that this was no game. What he had to say was deadly serious.

"Okay," he said, lowering the gun, but still keeping a tight hold on it. "This is the way it's going to shake down. Me and Angie here are gonna take a little walk. We're not going to be gone long—and we're not going far. If I hear any of you move a muscle, say a word, let out a fart…well, then I'm gonna see to it you're shut up for good. You understand that?''

Six heads moved up and down.

''I can't hear you.''

A murmured cacophony—*yes, sir.*

''Good.'' He let his gaze fall to each in turn. He wanted to pull off the damn stocking mask—he'd been wearing it for days—but he couldn't risk it. So he kept the stifling thing on. Soon, though. Soon, he'd be free again.

''One last thing,'' he added, standing up. ''If any of you tries anything funny, anything at all, Angie dies.'' He pointed at the old lady, the one who'd spent the last few hours huddled together with the young blonde Clive remembered seeing at the hostess stand. ''You don't want that on your conscience, do you?''

She shook her head and whispered, ''No.''

''I didn't think so.''

He glanced at the telephone sitting on the hostess stand. They'd called ten minutes ago, and Clive had once again refused to negotiate. That meant there were fifty minutes left before they were due to call again. He could put a lot of distance between himself and the cops in fifty minutes.

He walked backwards, tugging Angie with him. They had to get through the stairwell door and head down into the sub-basement. He hoped the cops had followed his instructions. He'd told them to stay the hell out of the basements, the lobby, the entire hotel. He'd said he'd know what they were up to because his team would tell him. And if he heard that the cops were close by, he'd start to feel antsy. If he felt antsy, he might get an itchy trigger finger. And if that happened, well, someone might die.

It was all bullshit, of course. He had no way in hell of knowing if they'd penetrated the basement, or anywhere else for that matter. But that was one reason he had Angie. His walking, talking insurance policy.

Her footsteps echoed in the stairwell, and he jerked her to a halt. "Take them off," he said, nodding toward her high-heeled shoes. Hell, he should have made her take them off long ago. Those heels were lethal. If she decided to attack, she could put out an eye.

Of course, she'd be stupid to try. After all, Clive had a gun trained on her back. Angie wasn't a stupid girl; she wouldn't do anything foolish. Even so, he jerked her upright when she started to bend down. She looked up, startled.

"Just kick them off," he said. "Keep your hands up here."

She complied in silence, kicking the shoes to the corner of the landing. He pushed her forward. "Keep moving."

She did, and they got to the utility room within five

minutes. Clive yanked the rope, stopping her. He pressed a hand against her shoulder. "Stay quiet," he said. And then Clive listened.

Silence.

All around him, beautiful silence. The cops hadn't come in, hadn't breached his perimeter.

Clive took a deep breath, realizing only then how tense he'd been merely from the possibility. But now...

Now freedom and a dingy gray wall loomed before him. Nothing could stop him now. Nothing and no one.

He relaxed his shoulder, letting the duffel fall to the ground. The clatter echoed through the empty room, and Angie jumped. Clive ignored her, unzipping the duffel to find the heavy mallet. Her eyes went wide when he lifted it, and she pressed her lips together until there was nothing left of her mouth except a thin line.

He moved toward her, and she jerked backwards. "Please. No." Her voice was hoarse, raspy.

Clive ignored her. A utility pipe protruded from the wall, and he tied her to it, like a dog staked in the backyard. Then he grasped the mallet, summoned the strength to lift it and get some momentum going, took aim, and swung.

DONOVAN HAD DRIVEN into Trenton that morning to meet with Joanie's parents. They'd talked to him twice by phone, and Joanie herself had called them, but he wanted to meet them in person. He thought it was the least he could do.

Of course, that meant he'd gotten stuck in some hellacious traffic, and now it was already well after noon and the heat was rising off the asphalt in waves. Despite the oppressive heat, the air around the staging area was charged, buzzing with activity and thick with anticipation. Something had happened, and Donovan wanted to know what.

He found Fisk in the thick of things, as usual. "What's the story?" Donovan asked.

Fisk held up a finger, then finished barking orders to a subordinate. When he turned to Donovan, his face was unreadable.

Donovan frowned, dread building in his gut. "What?"

"Our perp didn't answer the last contact call."

Donovan looked at his watch. One forty-five. Fifteen minutes until the next call. "And?"

"We're waiting. Gonna see what happens with the two o'clock call. But if he doesn't answer that one, we've got a SWAT team going in." Fisk looked at him, his expression grave. "One way or another, in twenty minutes we'll know one hell of a lot more than we do now."

THE DIM BEAM from Clive's flashlight barely cut through the pitch black of the ancient access tunnel.

In the distance, he could hear the unmistakable rush of water. Closer, he could hear the scurry of living things. It didn't matter. The dark, the creatures, none of it. Because they meant freedom. He'd been right. He'd done his research, and he'd found a way out.

"Wh—where are we?" Angie's voice was soft, and he knew she must really be terrified if her fear of the tunnels had overcome her fear of him. She'd been so afraid when he'd lifted the mallet to smash through the wall. He'd seen the fear in her eyes and it had given him power. It had been a test, of sorts. Now Clive knew that he could pull the trigger when he met Worthington face to face.

Now, though, he didn't have to. He had a better plan—Worthington had killed Emily. Now Clive would let Worthington see how it felt to be totally powerless to help someone.

"Old subway access tunnels," he said, answering her question. "They've been closed off for years." He'd learned about the entrance by accident when he was studying the building plans looking for the most direct way to the ground floor from the penthouse. He'd been bored, and had started digging a little deeper than he'd originally intended. The extra research had been worth it, though, when he'd found the access tunnel that connected to the sub-basement.

The access had long ago been walled over, but Clive had poked around and found the old tunnel entrance—right behind a wall of rotting drywall covered in mildewed white tile.

"What are we doing down here?" Her voice was still meek, and she held her bound wrists close to her chest in a self-protective gesture.

"I'm leaving," Clive said. "You're staying."

She drew in a shaky breath. "Please, please don't hurt me."

"Give me a reason not to."

"I—I don't know what you want."

"Just information, Angie. That's all. Just simple information."

She licked her lips, but nodded. Clive decided to take that as assent.

"The girl you took up in the elevator. She was going to see Mr. Worthington?"

Confusion flashed in Angie's eyes, but she answered. "Yes."

"A date?"

"I don't know." Clive didn't believe her, but it didn't matter. Considering the sexy little outfit, there was no doubt about the purpose of the blonde's visit.

"Who is she?"

"I—I don't know what you mean."

"Her *name,* Angie." He made a broad gesture with the gun. "Just tell me her name. That's easy, right?"

"J-Joan," she said, choking the word out. "I don't know her last name."

"Okay," Clive said. "We can work with that." He

patted her shoulder, ignoring the way she shrank from his touch. "You're doing great, Angie. Now tell me how you know her."

Angie didn't answer. He shined the light on her face, saw the tears streaming down her dust-stained cheeks.

"Chin up, Angie. It's almost over. Just a little bit more and then we go our separate ways. You'd like that, right?" He held up a hand. "It's okay, you won't hurt my feelings. Just tell me what I want to know and I'll leave you all alone. You tell me the truth, and you'll be fine. It's only if you lie that bad things will happen. Okay?"

A tiny nod.

"Good. Now tell me how you know her."

Angie's mouth moved, but only muffled tones came out.

Clive leaned in, trying to decipher the sounds. "Black floor?"

"Bookstore." The word was barely audible. She drew a deep breath. "She works at a bookstore in Gramercy Park. I don't remember the name."

That was good enough, and Clive exhaled. He had her now. "Excellent, Angie. You did great." He shined the flashlight down the path. "Let's go."

"I thought you were leaving me."

"Not in the dark with rats, Angie. I'm going to get you out in the light first."

She hesitated, but then turned to walk in the direction he'd pointed. He knew she would. She had no other choice. And as soon as she turned, he lashed out, the butt end of the gun cracking against the back of her head.

She crumpled into a heap on the damp, filthy floor.

Clive stepped over her. "Sleep tight, Angie," he said. He shone the beam of the flashlight into the dark. "And now, bookstore Joan, it's your turn."

12

JOAN WOKE UP in the circle of Bryce's arms, feeling like she'd always been there, and wishing that she never had to leave. Eventually, though, she knew that life would return to normal. And no matter how much she might wish it weren't so, having Bryce in bed with her definitely wasn't the norm.

With a little sigh, she slid carefully out of his embrace, then scooted to the edge of the bed. She slipped into the robe she now considered hers and padded barefoot to the kitchen area. They'd finished off the olives that morning—calling it breakfast—and then Bryce had done a bit of work before enticing her to have "lunch" in bed. He'd neglected to mention that no food would be involved.

Not that she'd minded, of course. But now she was hungry, and Joan knew one thing for certain—it was time to break open the bag of chocolate chip cookies.

Bryce wandered in as she was popping the first one into her mouth. Her heart lifted just from seeing his face, and Joan knew she was in trouble. She had it bad, all right. Somewhere over the course of the past few days she'd gone and fallen in love with Bryce Worthington.

She'd done some stupid things in her life, but this had to top the list. Because unless the gunman intended to hold the hostages for the next forty or fifty years, the odds were good that pretty soon the door to the penthouse would open and Bryce and Joan would go their separate ways.

It wasn't a future she looked forward to.

Bryce crossed the room and came to her side. He reached into the bag and pulled out a cookie, all the while looking at her curiously. "You okay?"

She managed a smile. "Fine," she said. "Just tired. You've worn me out."

"*I've* worn *you* out? Somehow I don't believe that."

"You're right," she said, shaking off her melancholy. "I've got energy to burn." She cocked her head toward the bedroom. "Think you can keep up with me?"

"I think I can give it a try." He took the bag of cookies. "First one naked gets the cookies?"

Joan laughed. "It's a bet."

He took her hand then, tugging her forward. His hands slid down to cup her butt, and he brushed a kiss over her ear.

"Bryce, I—" She cut herself off, not sure what she intended to say. She wanted to tell him how much he'd come to mean to her, how comfortable she felt around him, and how much she didn't want this to end. Somehow, though, she couldn't get the words to form.

"What is it?"

"I just—"

This time, it was a pounding at the door that interrupted her.

"Joan? It's Donovan."

Their eyes met, and instead of the rush of relief she should have felt, a deep sadness washed over her.

"Bryce?" Another voice. Joan didn't recognize it.

"Leo," Bryce said. "My attorney." He met her eyes, and for one brilliant, fabulous moment, she saw her own distress reflected on his face. She had the absurd impulse to grab his hand and run. But, of course, there was nowhere to run to.

And then Bryce headed for the foyer and the spell was broken. She tagged after him, holding her breath as he flipped the lock and opened the door to reveal Donovan and another man, each looking incredibly relieved.

Donovan rushed inside, clamping his hands on either of her shoulders. "Thank God, kid." He looked her in the eyes. "You okay?"

She nodded, feeling oddly bewildered. Beside her, the attorney had caught Bryce in a bear hug and was clapping him forcefully on the back.

"Perfect timing," he said. "Got a crisis in the New

Jersey deal, and you need to put in some face time. This couldn't have come at a better moment."

A crooked grin danced across Bryce's mouth. "Glad to see you too, Leo."

Leo, Joan noticed, had the good grace to look sheepish. "Sorry. But we've worked too hard on this deal for it to all blow up now."

Bryce caught Joan's eye. "The man's a slave driver."

She laughed, feeling absurdly pleased that he'd included her in the conversation with the attorney.

"Don't worry, Leo," Bryce said. "The deal's not going to fall through."

Joan turned to Donovan. "What happened?" she asked. "Did you catch him? Are the hostages okay?"

"The gunman escaped," Donovan said. He licked his lips. "Most of the hostages are fine," he said.

"Most?" She frowned. "But you said—"

"I know what I said, Joanie, and I'm sorry." He reached out, took her hand, and fear rose in her gut. "I know you, kid, and you would have driven yourself crazy with worry."

"So it wasn't okay. When you said it was under control, it wasn't."

He shook his head. "No." He drew in a breath, pain etched in the lines of his face. "And now one of the hostages is missing."

"Oh, God," Joan said, closing her eyes. The whole

situation was a nightmare, but even more so for that poor person.

"Joan," Donovan continued, squeezing her hand, "it's Angie."

She blinked, his words not making sense. "But...but I thought you said she'd clocked out."

He nodded. "She had. Apparently she was working off the clock."

Joan closed her eyes, the import of his words hitting her over the head. Angie had been working off the clock because of Joan. *Shit.*

Bryce's hand closed over her arm and she took a deep breath. It was the gunman. It was *his* fault.

"How's Kathy?" she asked. She knew she should be angry—hell, *furious*—with Donovan for keeping her in the dark, but somehow she couldn't work up the energy. She was numb. And, deep down, she knew he'd only wanted to protect her.

"As well as can be expected," Donovan said. "I think she'd like to see you."

"Of course." She turned blindly, wondering where her clothes were. She started toward the bedroom, but Bryce caught her hand. Startled, she stopped, then looked up into his eyes.

"She'll be okay," he said. "The other hostages are fine, and that's a good sign. He probably just took her along to make sure he got out without incident. Once he realizes the cops aren't tailing him, he'll let her go."

His words worked on her like a balm. "I hope so."

He didn't try to reassure her again, and she appreciated that. Instead, he just kissed her forehead. "Go see Kathy," he said. "I'm sure she needs you. You've got my cell number if you need it."

Joan nodded, feeling slightly dazed as she headed back into the bedroom to get dressed.

"And Joan," Bryce called. "If I don't see you before, we're still on for dinner on Friday, right?"

She nodded, unable to help the smile that crossed her face. "Right."

As she closed the louvered doors behind her, she hugged herself. They were back in the real world now, and still he'd remembered dinner at her parents' the next day. And to Joan, that was worth more than every touch and whisper they'd shared over the past three days.

Maybe fairy tales came true after all.

LEO PAUSED in the doorway of the conference room, looked at Bryce and shook his head. "I can't believe it. I just can't believe it."

For the tenth time since eight that morning, Bryce looked up from the pile of papers spread across the conference room table. He'd commandeered the large room the night before, needing a quiet place to work while he tried to get through the backlog of paperwork that had built up. He'd worked through the night, leaving the room only to use the gym and shower facilities the firm had installed on the thirty-eighth floor.

"I'm not going to finish this if you keep interrupting me," Bryce said. The truth was he was having a hell of a time concentrating even during those brief periods when Leo left him alone. Instead of work, his mind was filled with Joan. He wondered what she was doing—*how* she was doing. And he wondered if she was thinking of him.

They'd known each other for such a short period of time on a temporal scale, and yet in a lot of respects he felt closer to her than anyone.

Leo was still staring at him from the doorway, and Bryce sighed, then pulled his reading glasses off and tossed them on the table. "Talk," he said. "Get it out of your system."

Leo came in, then parked himself in one of the plush chairs that encircled the conference table. He leaned back, his hands steepled in his lap. After a moment, he released a world-weary sigh. Bryce just stared at him, the theatrics of Leo's performance starting to get under his skin.

"I think you should leave New York," Leo finally said. "We can finalize the deal in Texas."

Bryce regarded Leo for a moment. "You're serious."

"Hell yes," Leo said.

"Why?" In truth, Bryce had been thinking along the same lines himself, but he was curious about his attorney's reasoning. "Did you get used to not having me around?"

Leo ignored the joke, his expression not changing in the slightest.

Bryce sighed, then leaned back in his chair. "Okay, I'll bite. What's on your mind?"

"What's on my mind? Bryce, the cops have determined that you were this nut's target. It's only a matter of time before that maniac tries something again."

"He can try something in Texas, too." Bryce hadn't been surprised when the cops had given him their conclusion. They didn't know for sure, of course, but the hostages had been initially rounded up in the service hallway, right in front of the penthouse elevator. As the cops saw it, the odds were good that Bryce was the target, and that something had gone wrong.

It was a conclusion Bryce happened to agree with. He just didn't know what he should do about it. He hated the thought of turning his life upside down. Especially since he might be turning it upside down forever. The news reports had indicated that the gunman was at large, managing to evade police. Who knew how long he could stay on the lam, perpetually stalking Bryce.

Leo frowned. "I think the odds of this nutcase going all the way to Texas are slim. At the very least, you've already got alarms and dogs and all that shit in Austin. If you're there, it'll give the cops a chance to catch this guy."

Bryce had to admit that Leo's plan made sense. They'd managed to move the New Jersey deal forward, and now all that was left to tie up were the final stages of due diligence and some paperwork. The Carpenter deal was stalled in litigation. But other deals were bubbling, and the ones that were percolating the loudest were in Houston and Dallas. Life was moving forward again, but, for some inexplicable reason, Bryce was anchored in Manhattan while the current rushed past him.

No, not inexplicable. He knew the reason; he just didn't want to face it—Joan. In less than a week, she'd wriggled her way into his life. And, more than that, it felt right. It was a feeling that scared him, because he didn't trust it. Didn't trust the knot in his gut that said it was right, that what he had with Joan was good. He couldn't quite see past the wall he'd built up, a wall plastered with his mother's face, his father's crushing disappointment when his wife left him, and the sear of betrayal that had ripped through Bryce those many years ago.

He shook his head. He had every reason in the world to go back to Texas, to focus on his work and get on with his life. He wasn't looking for a commitment, didn't need a commitment, and he'd be damned if he'd confuse the passion borne of forced intimacy for that foolish fantasy known as true, lasting love.

Bryce played for keeps, and he knew well enough that love wasn't that kind of game. No, in business he knew the rules, knew how to play, and knew how to win. But love? Even with a woman like Joan, in the end, it was a losing battle. And Bryce never bet against the house.

Leo had been watching him in silence, but now he spoke. "You know I'm right."

Bryce shook away his thoughts, then looked at his friend. "I know a lot of things. That doesn't mean I always do them."

"You've never done a stupid thing in your life," Leo said. "Don't start now. Not when it could get you killed."

The intercom buzzed before Bryce could answer, and the thirtieth-floor receptionist announced a call for Bryce. He picked up the handset, recognizing the thick, gravelly voice of the detective who'd been assigned to track down the gunman. He put the call on speaker.

"Leo's here," Bryce said. "I've got you on speaker."

"Mr. Worthington, Mr. Tucker," the detective said, "I've got some disturbing news."

Bryce met Leo's eyes. *Here it comes.* "We're listening."

"We've confirmed our suspicion that Mr. Worthington was the target."

"Confirmed how?" Leo asked.

"Interviews with the hostages," the detective said. "Apparently our gunman had slightly loose lips. He didn't name anyone specifically, but there was enough information to make it almost a certainty that he was after Mr. Worthington."

"Any idea who the guy is?" Bryce asked. "Or if he really did have partners?"

"At this point, we believe he was working alone, but we haven't been able to confirm that. There was no other gunman with the hostages, that we know for sure." He paused, and Bryce heard him sifting through some papers.

"As for who he is," the detective continued, "we're looking into that, as well. Mr. Tucker allowed us access to the file he keeps regarding harassment, and we've crossed that with some individuals at Carpenter Shipping. Right now that seems a likely possibility. We've also pulled a few other letters—one fellow in California's wife died after a layoff. Cancer, and she didn't have insurance. The ironic thing is that the guy was on the company's list to get fired, anyway. So the takeover didn't have anything to do with his problems. But we're trying to track his whereabouts, since his letters suggest he's placed the blame anywhere but on himself." He paused. "Bits and pieces, but no solid leads yet. As I said, Carpenter

Shipping seems the most likely. It's timely, and the shareholders are none too happy.''

Bryce nodded. ''All right,'' he said. ''Keep me posted.''

''Of course.'' The detective cleared his throat. ''At the present, we think it would be advisable for you to leave New York. Do you think you could arrange that?''

Bryce met Leo's eyes. For a second, he said nothing. Then he took a deep breath. ''Yes,'' he finally said. ''I think that can be arranged.''

They finished up with the detective in short order, and Bryce walked with Leo back to his office. ''I'll have Lilly book you on the next flight out,'' Leo said.

Bryce rubbed his temples. ''If it's all the same to you,'' he said, ''I'd like to pack.'' He also needed to say goodbye to Joan.

Leo had the good grace to look a little sheepish. ''Sorry. I just want to get you the hell out of here.''

''I'm going,'' Bryce said. ''But I'm going to the hotel first, and then I'm going to take Joan to lunch.'' Since he was going to miss dinner, it was, he figured, the least he could do. They needed to talk, too.

Bryce knew that leaving for Texas was the right thing. The woman was too tempting, and Bryce wasn't in a position to succumb to temptation. Of course, none of that would make his departure any easier.

Leo's face hardened.

''What?'' Bryce demanded.

''You need to go *now.*''

''Leo...''

Leo held up both hands, as if warding off his client's wrath. ''I just don't want you to do something stupid. You've got more than just yourself to think of, you know. You get nailed by some psychopath, and it's not just you that's dead, it's Worthington Industries.''

''I think the company can keep chugging on without me,'' Bryce said dryly. ''I'd like to believe my employees were hired for their competence.''

''Oh, the company will survive, but what about the public offering? It won't happen, and a lot of your shareholders will end up losing one hell of a lot of money.''

With that, Bryce couldn't argue. If Bryce weren't in the picture, the offering wouldn't go forward. Maybe in a few years, after the company had time to regroup. But not right then. ''I have no intention of putting the company at risk,'' he said. ''Tell Lilly she can book me on the four-fifty flight.''

''Will do,'' Leo said.

Bryce's cell phone rang, and he pulled it out of his pocket. *Joan.* ''Hey,'' he said, ''I was just going to call you.''

''B-Bryce.'' Her voice broke, and he could hear her fighting back tears.

Fear crashed over him, his body tensing. "Joan? What is it?"

"Angie. They found her."

"Oh, God." He closed his eyes, fearing the worst.

"No, no." She spoke hastily, then drew in a breath. "She's alive. But she's unconscious. Oh, Bryce. They found her in the subway tunnels. In the dark."

"Where are you?"

"I'm at the hospital. With Kathy."

He made a note as she gave him the details. "I'll meet you there."

JOAN SAT on a bench in the hallway outside of Intensive Care. Angie had some cranial bleeding, and she was under observation, but the prognosis was good. With any luck, she'd be transferred to another floor within the day.

None of which made Joan feel any better. And so she sat on the bench while Kathy sat with Angie, waiting for the only person who might possibly lift her spirits.

The elevator dinged, and Joan looked up, her pulse quickening as the doors slid open. A nurse in flowered scrubs stepped off, and Joan sighed, fighting a rush of disappointment. Another ding, and the doors to the second elevator slid open and, this time, there he was. Joan released a breath in a whoosh, so relieved she feared her knees wouldn't hold her if she stood up.

His gaze scanned the hallway, finding her. And

then he smiled. A smile of apology and encouragement and hope.

Joan ran to him, tears streaming down her face as she buried her head in his shoulder.

"Hey, hey, it's okay. Everything's going to be fine." He made soft soothing sounds, his hand stroking her back, his lips pressing kisses to the top of her head. "I talked to the duty nurse," he murmured. "Angie is doing great."

Joan nodded. "I know." They expected her to regain consciousness within the next twenty-four hours. Right then, the painkillers alone were probably keeping her knocked out more than her injuries. "It's not that. I mean, it is, but—"

He tilted her chin up, looking into her eyes. "This is not your fault."

She melted against him, her body sagging in relief simply because he'd said it out loud. She knew that, really she did. She just didn't *know* it. "If I hadn't used her to get to you…"

"By that logic, it's my fault because I didn't show up for our dinner date. Do you believe that?"

She shook her head. "No. I know you're right. It's just…" She trailed off, shaking her head.

"You feel like there's nothing you can do, and you hate it."

Again, he'd nailed it. "Yeah." She took a deep breath and put her hands on his shoulders, lifting up on her toes to kiss his cheek. "Thanks."

He stroked her face, his eyes reflecting a sadness that seemed out of place. "Anytime," he whispered.

"Bryce?"

The sadness disappeared, and his eyes turned serious. "Joan," he said, "we need to talk."

She frowned, not certain what he wanted to talk about, but knowing it couldn't be good. She nodded. "All right."

They ended up in the hospital cafeteria, each nursing a cup of bitter coffee. He'd been silent on the trip down, and Joan hadn't pushed. Now, though, she wanted to know what was going on. "Bryce, what is it?"

"I'm leaving for Texas at five," he said.

"Oh." She blinked, struggling for comprehension. "My mom really wanted to meet you."

"I'm sorry about that. I wanted to meet your parents, too. But it turns out I was the target. The police think it's best if I go."

He spoke so matter-of-factly that it took a few moments for his words to register. "You?" she finally said. "I don't understand."

"In my business, I anger a lot of people. Layoffs, any number of things, can trigger someone unstable."

"You're talking like it's no big deal," she said, trying to keep the frantic tone out of her voice. "It's a huge deal."

His expression took on a hard edge. "Believe me, babe, I know that. That's why I'm leaving."

She wanted to stay cool, to discuss this like a reasonable person, but all she could do was think that she really was losing him. A tear trickled down her cheek, and she angrily brushed it away, cursing herself for believing even a little in fairy tales.

He reached out, brushing the pad of his thumb under her eye. "I'm sorry," he said.

"I…I'm going to miss you. I don't want you to go away." She blurted the words out without thinking. "Oh, God. I didn't mean that. I want you to be safe."

A thin smile touched his lips. "I appreciate that."

"I just…" She pressed her lips together, gathering courage. "I was hoping that we could see each other some more." She shrugged. "See if maybe this thing between us can go somewhere in the real world."

"Oh, sweetheart." He took both her hands in his, then pressed a kiss to her thumbs. "I don't know how to say this without hurting you, and I really don't want to hurt you."

Joan felt cold, and she pulled back, clutching her coffee cup between her hands. "It's okay. I shouldn't have said anything. I should know better than to think there could be anything real between us. You're fantasy material, Bryce Worthington. And even though I have an ego, I'm smart enough to know that I'm not the kind of girl a guy like you ends up with."

A flash of anger crossed his face. "You've never talked about yourself like that," he said. "Don't start now."

"I'm not being self-deprecating, Bryce. I'm just stating facts. If I'm wrong, then tell me."

"You're wrong," he said, lighting a spark of hope in her. "I care about you, Joan. More deeply than I would have imagined or, frankly, thought possible."

Her heart skipped a beat.

"But in the end it doesn't change anything." His words held a note of sadness, as if they cut up his insides as much as they destroyed hers.

"I don't understand."

"I can't be in a relationship, Joan."

"Why not?"

"My business. My life. It's a twenty-four-hour gig. You know that. You saw just the tiniest slice of how it is. And I'm not looking to get tied down. Not now, maybe not ever."

She opened her mouth, planning to say all sorts of things about how she'd wait until he was ready and in the meantime she'd be there for him. But she couldn't say it. She didn't want to be the woman he slept with when he came to New York. She wanted all of him, or she didn't want him at all.

The trouble was she *did* want him. She just couldn't have him.

"So that's it?" she said, struggling to keep the anger out of her voice. "The great CEO has spoken and issued his edict. No relationship. End of story. That's the way this plays out?"

"It's not the kind of decision we can make together, Joan. I can either be with you or I can't. Nothing you can do can change that.''

She drew in a breath. ''So you're just going to leave. You tell me that you care about me and then you're just going to walk away?''

''I'm sorry,'' he said.

She flinched. ''That's not good enough.''

He met her eyes. ''I know. For that, I'm sorry, too.''

13

EVEN HER MOM'S meat loaf wasn't helping.

Joan sighed, picking at the food on her plate. Her mom got up to pull a pie out of the oven, and on her way back to the table, she gave Joan a quick hug.

"He's an idiot," her father said. "I don't care how much money he has, the man's an idiot."

Joan rolled her eyes. "He's not, Daddy."

She'd told them everything—well, not *everything*—but enough that her parents knew she'd fallen hard for the likes of Bryce Worthington. It had helped, actually, talking through it with them. Her parents had such a strong relationship, and part of that, she knew, came from the fact that they were so grounded in the real world. They had an honesty and a moral code that she valued. That she didn't want to lose. How on earth would she have been able to keep that code if she was with Bryce, with millions of dollars suddenly at her disposal?

But that was a stupid argument and she knew it. Bryce had started out as working-class and his integrity was intact. Sure, he dated a lot of women—Joan had gone on a Bryce Worthington reading binge that afternoon—but the articles all made clear what a down-to-earth guy he was. Some of the articles even talked about his charitable work, which was far more extensive than he'd let on when he described the work he did for Habitat for Humanity.

No, Joan couldn't even say that Bryce walking away was all for the best. It wasn't for the best. It sucked. And what really sucked was that she didn't know how to get him back. Because unless he was lying to her, this wasn't even about her. It was about him and his drive and how much he was able to give to a relationship.

Joan couldn't change him. Hell, she couldn't even try.

"Well," her mother said brightly, "I made apple pie."

"Great," Joan said. "That should fix everything."

Her parents laughed, and Joan joined in. For every crisis in her life, from bad grades to bad boyfriends, her mom had always been there with pie. It had become almost a tradition. It never helped, of course, but it certainly never hurt, either.

She looked up at her mom. "I'll take a slice now, please."

At the moment, she could use all the pie she could get.

HORNS BLARED and tires squealed as the early morning traffic wended its way through Gramercy Park.

From the café across the street, Clive watched the bookstore, unable to help the smile that spread across his face. Angie had told him the truth, and for two days now, he'd been watching. Biding his time and planning.

The storefront was a wall of windows, revealing a display of books in the window. A counter with a cash register was set up past that, and right then Joan was chatting with a customer. Even from across the street he could see her, her blond hair shining in the overhead lights.

Bitch.

Soon. Very, very soon.

He'd worked it all out in his head, and he knew he needed to act quickly. He had wanted to move even faster, but the girl had disappeared. So he'd taken a chance, going into the bookstore and overhearing Angie's sister on the phone. Angie was recovering, but didn't remember anything of the night Clive had clubbed her. Good. Joan had left for New Jersey to spend the weekend with her parents until the store opened again on Tuesday. Bad.

At least, though, Clive knew she was coming back.

He used the extra time to his advantage. He'd learned that Joan lived in the apartment above the bookstore. And he'd learned, as well, that the building had a fire escape in the back that Joan used as a balcony. Most likely, she kept her windows locked, stopping anyone from getting in by the fire escape. But

Clive knew he could buy glass cutters at any hardware store.

No, Joan's windows weren't a problem. Worthington, however, was. And it was that problem that Clive now pondered as he watched Joan through the window. The man had left New York. Clive hadn't expected that, though he had to admit he should have seen it coming.

Which raised the million-dollar question—how much did Worthington care about Joan Benetti?

Clive drummed his fingers on his thigh. He didn't know. But he *did* know that Worthington would protect his reputation. If it got out that he alone could prevent the death of an innocent woman…

Clive smiled. He'd take Joan. And once he had her, he'd tell Worthington just how much it would cost to get her back.

Yes. Yes, that would work. That would get Worthington's attention. He'd demand ransom first, and *then* he'd kill her.

BRYCE HOISTED the ax and brought it down, burying the blade deep in the upturned log. The wood split along the grain, the two sections each falling to the side. With the back of his left hand, he wiped the sweat from his brow. Over ninety-five degrees in Austin, and he'd been at this for more than an hour.

Across the yard, Leo eyed him from the comfort of the porch. The attorney had flown into Austin the day before, and they'd been up for over twenty-four hours working on two new deals.

Leo raised his beer, his eyes tired. "You realize you've got a few months until you'll be needing firewood," his friend shouted, then popped the top on a fresh beer. "Or is there something else you're working through? I know it's not these deals. We got all the kinks worked out this morning."

With a scowl, Bryce tossed the ax into the grass, his shoulders and back aching. He reached down and grabbed his beer from where he'd left it on the ground. He took a long swallow, downing the rest of the cool liquid, then left the empty can on the tree stump.

"Well?" Leo prodded.

"Not something," Bryce admitted, walking the length of the manicured yard to join his friend on the porch. "Someone."

For days now, his thoughts had been filled with little more than work and Joan. And lately, instead of lessening, the thoughts of Joan were increasing, pushing aside work until Bryce was actually having trouble focusing on his pending deals.

"Joan," Leo said. He shook his head, the gesture almost fatherly. "I wanted you to find a woman. I didn't think you'd do it so damn fast. I hear wedding bells, my friend. Marj is going to be thrilled."

Bryce shook his head. "Come on, Leo. You know me. I'm not interested in getting married—in even having a serious relationship—unless I can give it my all. It's not fair to her and it's not fair to me."

"As your attorney and your friend, I have only one response to that—bullshit."

Bryce glared at his friend, but didn't argue. Instead, he reached down for a rock, eyed the can on the stump, took aim, and threw. *Smack!* Bull's-eye. The can went tumbling.

"No married person on the planet gives marriage their all," Leo said, sticking to the topic at hand. "Everybody always has something else in their life. Or they should. That's what's called well-rounded."

Bryce rolled his eyes at the note of sarcasm in Leo's voice. "It's one thing to have other interests. It's another to be completely absorbed by your work to the detriment of your relationship."

"So don't be."

Bryce raised an eyebrow. "My self-absorption is what pays your hourly rate."

Leo grinned. "I think I can rustle up a few new clients if you back off a little."

With a sigh, Bryce sat at the table. "I've got obligations," he said. Even as he spoke, though, he knew he was only making excuses. He'd never been afraid of anything in his life. But he was afraid of this. Afraid of failing at love because it could blind-side him. He wouldn't see the end coming, just like he hadn't seen his mother's betrayal coming. And how the hell did you fight something that insidious if it came silently in the night?

"We make our own priorities," Leo said. "Hell, you should know that better than anyone."

"That's my point," Bryce said. "The company is my priority. Right now it has to be. If I don't focus, I'll lose out on the chance to make millions."

Leo nodded. "That's probably true. But you already have millions."

"That's not the point, and you know it. Taking the company public could make a lot of people who work for me very, very wealthy. They have mortgages to pay. Families to support. And they've been working hard toward this."

"You know my position, Bryce. I think you'll be better off taking the company public with a wife. But either way, I think you need to step back and look at the larger picture."

Bryce scowled. "What picture is that?"

"You told me yourself—you've hired good people who know how to do their jobs. So why are you in this so deep? Because, I have to wonder, when you get to the point where the job becomes your life, is it really worth it?"

Bryce opened his mouth and then closed it again. What he'd told Leo was true. The company could go on without him.

"She's good for you, Bryce," Leo said softly. "I don't know what happened between you two in that penthouse, but I do know that she's crept into every one of our conversations. And when you're not talking about her, you're thinking about her. There's a look in your eye, my friend. I know. It's the same look I have when I think about Marj. Even to this day—even after twenty-eight years of marriage."

"That long? I had no idea. Congratulations."

Leo nodded. "Thanks."

He wanted to ask Leo if he was afraid. Afraid that now that the relationship was comfortable that she'd pull the rug out from him and go. But Bryce didn't ask. He didn't ask because he knew the answer—Leo had no such fears.

And that's when it hit him. That's when he *knew*. He wasn't afraid, either. The fear had evaporated, leaving only a bone-deep sadness that his mother had left. But nothing more. The woman had shadowed his life long enough. It was time Bryce said goodbye once and for all.

Sure, he knew that Joan *might* leave someday. He also knew that the moon might drop out of the sky and fall to earth. But he didn't believe it. Because he knew in his heart—no, he knew in his *soul*—that Joan loved him. And that she'd never, ever do anything to hurt him.

So help him, he loved her, too. And he couldn't wait to get back to New York to tell her in person. He hoped like hell that he still had a chance with her. That somehow, by being an idiot at the hospital, he hadn't completely blown the most important deal of his life.

14

JOAN KICKED HER FEET up on the coffee table and clicked the power button on the television's remote control. Ronnie's TV sprang to life, the familiar morning show theme music filling the apartment.

Joan snuggled into the pillows. Thank God for television and coffee. Without them, she'd be a zombie for half the day instead of just half an hour.

She stared blankly at the television for a few minutes, her mind actually clicking into gear when the financial segment came on. She had to grin. Thanks to Bryce, this was no longer the part of the show she tuned out.

In fact, since Bryce had left, she'd made a habit of watching the financial news across a variety of networks. It wasn't helping her melancholy in the least, but she was getting a good feel for how the NASDAQ worked. And, for some inexplicable reason, she couldn't go a day anymore without hearing some bit of news about the business world. Missing it was like giving up. So long as she tuned in faithfully, she could keep alive the illusion that Bryce had come back for her.

Stupid, maybe, but there you go.

The local weather was just coming on—hot, no surprise there—when the buzzer sounded. Frowning, Joan went to the intercom. "Yes?"

"Joan, it's Donovan. Buzz me up."

She did, hitting the button that operated the lock on the back stairs. The back entrance circumvented the store and led straight to the two interior apartments. She waited a few minutes, then unlocked the door, opening it just as he stepped onto the fourth-floor landing.

"Morning," she said, stepping back to let him enter. "Does this mean you guys caught the creep?"

Donovan's shoulders moved in something resembling a shrug. "Not exactly," he said.

Joan stopped, something in Donovan's voice catching her attention. "What? What's happened?"

He took a deep breath, then pulled a paper clip out of his pocket. He twisted it between his fingers as he spoke. "Angie's doing better," he said. "She's starting to remember what happened the night of the escape."

Joan waited, her whole body tense.

"He wanted to know about you, Joan."

She squinted, Donovan's words not making sense. "Me? I don't understand. Why would he want—"

"We think you're the next target, kiddo." Donovan's voice was flat, the unemotional tone of a professional. His eyes told a different story, however. His eyes reflected pure fear.

Donovan was afraid for her. And that scared Joan most of all.

PATTI, BRYCE'S ASSISTANT, placed a stack of documents on his desk. "The ticket's on top," she said. "You're on the first flight back in the morning." She smiled broadly. "Do you want me to send flowers? Have you called to let her know you're coming?"

Bryce laughed. He'd hired Patti eight years ago, and the woman knew him inside and out. "Thanks, Pat, but I'm going to surprise her."

She beamed. "This is just so romantic," she murmured. The phone rang, and she leaned over, the picture of efficiency, to answer the extension on his desk. He tuned out the conversation until she punched the hold button and passed him the handset. "It's for you. A detective from New York."

"Thanks," Bryce said, taking the call. He expected Fisk's voice telling him they'd caught the gunman. Instead, he got Detective Donovan.

"Joan doesn't know I'm calling," Donovan said, skipping the usual polite preliminaries.

Bryce sat up, instantly on alert. "What is it? What's wrong?"

"Joan," Donovan said. "We believe she's our perp's next target."

Bryce was on his feet, not thinking, just reacting. "I'll be there by four," he said. He'd planned to fly commercial, but this meant a change of plans. He'd take the corporate jet.

"You may still be a target, too," Donovan said. "I can't recommend that you come up here. We've got her under police protection. I just thought that you should know."

"I'm coming to her," Bryce said, not mentioning that he'd planned to come anyway. "If there's some way you have of preventing me from entering the city, tell me now. Otherwise I'm heading to the airport." He took a breath. "And tell Joan to pack," he added. "I'm bringing her home."

IDIOTS.

The police had apparently figured out that Clive had his eye on Joan, and for that he gave them some credit. But their idea of police protection was sadly, sadly lacking. There was one patrol officer in a car on the street, and another walking a beat.

Not good enough. Not at all.

The apartment above Joan's shared a fire escape with hers, and it was vacant. And at the moment, Clive was camped out in the empty living room, waiting for darkness to fall. Waiting for Joan to come upstairs from the bookstore. Waiting for her to go to sleep.

But he wouldn't be waiting much longer. Soon, he'd be the one in control. And soon, Emily could rest in peace.

JOAN WAS NEAR the back of the store reshelving books when the little bell jingled. At first, she had to fight a wave of fear, but then she remembered the cop that Donovan had posted in the store's armchair. Joan thought it was probably overkill, but she wasn't about to say no to a guy whose sole purpose in life was to protect her butt.

"Give a shout if you need anything," she finally said. "I'll be right out."

"Actually," a familiar voice answered, "you do have something I need."

Joan spun around, almost knocking over the stack of books at her feet. Her hand flew to her mouth and she fought back tears. He'd come back. Bryce had come back.

In a rush, she maneuvered the stacks, emerging behind the cop. Bryce was by the counter, and she launched herself into his arms, delighted when he returned her embrace with equal enthusiasm.

"You came back," she said.

He held her tighter. "Of course," he said. "I came to get you."

Joan frowned, then leaned back to look at his face. "What are you talking about?"

"Home," he said. "With me."

She blinked and shook her head.

"I'm taking you with me. You'll be safer in Texas. Let the cops do their job."

"*Safer* with you? Last I heard, this nutcase was after you, too."

"As far as we know, the nutcase is in New York," Bryce countered. "And my house is as secure as any house can be."

Joan glanced toward the seated cop who was watching them with interest. She considered asking him to leave, and then decided not to bother. At the moment, her emotions were a jumble of anger, confusion and relief. There simply wasn't any room for embarrassment.

"I don't want to go to Texas," she said.

"Joan, don't be stupid."

"Stupid," she repeated. "*Stupid?* I've already been that." She drew in a breath, pulling out of his embrace to pace the room. "I heard your voice, and I thought you came back for me. For us."

"I am," he said. "I did."

She shook her head. "No, you didn't. You're here because some lunatic decided you were too hard to get. I'm sloppy seconds, thank you very much, and you're feeling guilty."

"No."

She crossed her arms over her chest, wanting to believe him, but not quite able to. "Prove it."

He was at her side in two long strides. "I love you, Joan."

She squeezed her eyes shut, wishing she could block out the words. "Do you?" she whispered. She'd wanted to hear those words so badly. And now that he was finally saying them, she couldn't believe him. "How come you love me now when you didn't love me on Friday?"

"I've loved you from the first moment I saw you," he said. "I was stupid. I was scared of the risks. But you're worth the risk, sweetheart." He took her hands. "Be mad at me if you want, but don't punish us both because I was an idiot."

"I'm in danger," she said. "And suddenly you appear."

"Isn't that what knights on white horses are supposed to do?"

She fought the smile that touched her lips. "I suppose it is," she agreed. "But I don't want you to be with me out of guilt or some misguided sense of chivalry. I want—"

"I want you," Bryce interrupted. "I don't know how to make it any plainer. I've been hollow without you, Joan. Empty. You fill me up, and that's what I came to tell you. Our little gunman friend is just an inconvenience. That whole nightmare will be over soon, but I want the two of us to go on for the rest of our lives."

She blinked back tears. He'd said all the right things, drawn her in. And damned if she didn't believe him. "Did you just make that up?"

He shrugged. "I thought a little on the plane. I like to be prepared." His grin zinged down to her toes. "Please, Joan. Tell me you love me."

"I love you," she said without hesitation.

"Then come with me."

She hesitated only briefly, but then nodded. Not only did she love Bryce, but she trusted him implicitly. And if he said he loved her and wanted her with him, she had to believe him.

She smiled to herself, thinking about his various stock tips.

"What?" he asked.

"I was just thinking that, in the end, I'm following your advice—going with something relatively low risk that should pay out dividends in the coming years."

"A lot of dividends," Bryce confirmed. He kissed the tip of his finger and pressed it to her nose, then winked at the cop in the armchair. "I promise you're making an investment you definitely won't regret."

BRYCE HAD COME IN a private jet, and Joan had to admit that the idea of flying down to Texas in the thing intrigued her. She considered changing clothes for the occasion, but decided that was stupid. Instead, she rummaged in her bedroom closet, pulling out a few outfits to take. She didn't expect to be down there for more than a week, and Bryce had already told her it was hot. So, for the most part, she was filling her suitcase with shorts and tank tops.

Bryce was in the kitchen pouring them each a glass of wine. A toast. They were going to toast their life together. She couldn't wait. In fact, she was so gloriously, giddily happy that she almost forgot the cause of their whirlwind trip to Austin—a maniacal gunman out to get her and Bryce.

She shook her head, banishing the thoughts. They'd be fine. Donovan had told her the cops had some leads, and he'd assigned a whole cadre of officers to watch her. Even now, one was outside her front door and another was on the street below. The cops would tail her and Bryce to the airport, and once in Austin she and Bryce would head to his house. The way he described it, they'd be quite safe there.

She took one last glance around the room, trying to figure out if she'd left anything. She was a lousy packer, even worse when she had to do it on the spur of the moment.

It was when her gaze was drifting over the room that she noticed the window. Frowning, she stared at it, trying to figure out what was bugging her. And then she realized. Night had fallen, and the window was reflecting back the room's interior. Everywhere except for one small round section near the latch.

In a split second, she realized that someone had cut the glass away. In that same instant, she spun, ready to run from the room.

That's when she saw him.

He was standing in the bathroom, a stocking covering his face and a gun trained on her. "I'd stay quiet if I were you, Ms. Benetti." She nodded, and he gestured her toward the door. "Convenient of you to bring Mr. Worthington to your apartment. And so very considerate from my perspective."

He moved to her side, pressing the gun to her back. "You'll behave, I hope. I'd hate to have to kill you."

A shiver racked her body, and she nodded. "Whatever you want," she whispered. Her entire body felt cold. Numb. And she idly wondered if a person could get frostbite from fear.

"Good. Just so we understand each other." He poked her in the back. "Move."

He was urging her forward toward the bedroom door. Joan moved on shaky legs. They were almost to the door, and for some reason that made Joan feel better. Bryce was on the other side of that door. And even though there was nothing he could do—even though he couldn't make the gun at her temple disappear—just knowing he was there made her feel better. She couldn't die now. Not when she'd just found Bryce. Not when they'd proclaimed their love.

Somehow, someway, she knew it would all work out.

It had to.

BRYCE POURED a glass of merlot for himself, and was just about to set it down and pour a glass for Joan when her voice, barely a whisper, drifted in from behind him. ''Bryce...''

He turned—his eyes widening with disbelief. The glass tumbled from his fingers to shatter on the hardwood floor. In the doorway to the bedroom, the gunman held Joan around the waist, a pistol to her head.

Bryce felt a wave of nausea. *Please, God, don't let this madman hurt her.*

''Mr. Worthington,'' the man said, ''I'm so glad you're here. I've got an academic question for you.''

Fear flowed through Bryce as thick as blood. ''Yes?'' He had to try twice to get the word out past his bone-dry lips and tongue.

''How much will you pay? How much will you pay to keep the bitch alive?''

''Whatever you want,'' Bryce said, his voice barely audible. ''Just put the gun down.''

''You'll pay?''

''Yes,'' Bryce said.

''Whatever I want?''

''Yes.'' His eyes met Joan's and the fear he saw there reflected his own. ''Just don't hurt her.''

''You'll *pay?*''

Bryce swallowed, his mind going a thousand miles a minute. Something in the man's voice had changed. A slight alteration. Shifting somehow from greedy to nefarious. From unbalanced to evil.

He clenched his fist, forcing himself not to do anything foolish. *Where the hell were the cops?*

"You know what?" the man asked, his voice rising. "I don't give a fuck about the money. It's not about the money." His speech was speeding up. The man was stumbling over his words. Losing control.

Bryce's eyes darted around the room. He needed to do something, but there wasn't anything to do, not without risking Joan's life.

"It's all about money to you, though, isn't it? That's all that matters to you." He'd stepped slightly away from Joan, loosened his grip on her just as he'd lost his grip on reality. "How much would you have paid to save Emily?"

Bryce blinked. "Emily?"

"You son of a bitch," the man said, pure hatred lacing his voice. "You never cared about her. You didn't give a flip about her."

"I—" Bryce pressed his mouth closed, afraid that anything he said would set the guy off. He shifted slightly, his eyes going automatically to the window. The interior of the apartment was reflected back, but he thought he saw a movement. A cop? Donovan?

"You're scum, you know that? Scum. And so's your little bitch whore."

Bryce's eyes met Joan's, saw her fear, but also determination. And then he glanced toward the window. Her brow furrowed, and then she too looked toward the window. Her eyes widened just slightly, and Bryce knew she'd seen what he saw.

The only question was, what good would it do? The cops wouldn't rush the place, not if it would endanger Joan. And as long as the gun was trained on Joan, she was in danger.

Except the gun wasn't pressed to her skin anymore. If she dove to the floor the cops would have a split second to nail the son of a bitch.

Bryce silently cursed himself. Not only would it be impossible to tell Joan to dive, but it would be impossible to tell the cops to fire when she did.

He took a step forward, his attention caught by the glass paperweight on the coffee table. If only…

The man was still talking about Emily, his ramblings incoherent. All Bryce could discern was that the woman had died. And, he knew, so would he and Joan if Bryce didn't act fast. The man was disintegrating. Bryce didn't know why, but he could guess that he was the reason. The gunman had some fixation on him, and now that they were face to face—now that the guy had finally reached the moment he'd been waiting for—he was snapping.

But there was one thing—one tiny thing—that worked in their favor. As he disintegrated, he was keeping less and less of an eye on Joan.

Bryce swallowed, hating to take the risk, but knowing it was the only choice.

He counted to three, gathering his courage, and then turned to the window, yelling, "Police!"

As he'd hoped, the gunman turned in the same direction, his gun pointed at the window.

In the same instant, Bryce yelled, hollering for Joan to get down as he grabbed the paperweight.

Almost immediately, the gunman turned back, the gun arcing toward Bryce. But by then Bryce had thrown the heavy glass ball, his aim dead-on. He hit the guy in the wrist and the gun went flying. The gunman collapsed to the ground.

At the same moment, the glass window shattered, and Donovan leaped through. "Joan, Bryce! Damn, but that was stupid, you lucky bastard." Then he laughed and added, "Good shot."

Bryce barely heard him. He was too busy crawling to Joan. She was doing the same, and when she reached him, she threw her arms around him. He clutched her close, breathing in her scent, happier than he could ever remember being simply because they were alive.

"Joan. Joan, oh, baby."

Behind them, the gunman groaned. Out of the corner of his eye, Bryce saw him sit up, a hand to his head as Donovan bent to bind him with handcuffs. He jerked his arm away, reaching in his waistband and pulling out another gun.

Joan screamed and Bryce threw himself on her, knocking her onto the floor and shielding her with his body. It didn't matter. It was all over. The gunman never got off a shot. But Donovan did. And as the report still echoed in the room, Bryce lifted his head just enough to see the gunman's body sprawled on the hardwood floors.

"Oh, God, Bryce." Joan clung to him, tears racking her body. He held her close, saying soothing things, saying anything to make her feel better.

When the tears subsided, he shifted her in front of him, holding her shoulders as he looked deep in her eyes. "I love you, Joan. I love you, and I want you with me. Now and forever."

A weak grin touched her lips and she started crying all over again. But somehow, between the tears, she managed one simple word. "Yes."

Behind them, Donovan withdrew the gunman's wallet. "Clive Masterson," he said, then nodded. "I recognize that name. His wife died after he got laid off. Cancer. Couldn't get insurance."

Bryce ran a hand through his hair. He couldn't empathize with a madman who killed or took hostages out of some perverse desire for revenge, but he did understand the overpowering love that had driven him.

A deep sadness washed over him, and he took one last look at the body before turning away and pulling Joan close. "Forever," he said simply, the word both a prediction and a promise.

Joan hugged him tight, pressing her cheek to his chest as she murmured her response. "Forever." She pushed back, looking him in the eye. "Forever, and a day."

Epilogue

THE MORNING SUNLIGHT STREAMED in through the window, filling the bedroom with ribbons of light. In bed, Joan stretched and glanced at the clock, her eyes going wide when she saw the time. Already after nine! How on earth had she slept so late?

She threw the covers aside and started scrambling out of bed, silently cursing Bryce for not waking her up before he left for the airport. He knew she had to open the store this morning, and after three months of marriage, he should also know that she could sleep through the blare of alarm clocks with ease.

Okay, okay. She'd make it. Sure. No problem. She'd just throw on a skirt, splurge on a taxi, and still get to the store by ten.

With a little smile, she headed for the bathroom, remembering that the taxi wasn't a splurge anymore. Bryce kept telling her that someday she'd get used to the size of their bank account, but so far she didn't believe him. Heck, they'd been living in the Fifth Avenue apartment for almost four months now, and she still wasn't used to anything about it. Not the size, not the doorman, and certainly not the Central Park view.

She took a quick shower, tossed on a robe and headed back into the bedroom to change. What she saw there made her stop in her tracks—Bryce, on the bed, with a jar of olives.

"A picnic," he said.

She laughed. "What are you doing here? I thought you had to go to Atlanta today."

"Nope," he said, looking rather smug. "I told a little fib."

She lifted an eyebrow as she crawled onto the bed. "Oh, really?"

"Do you know what today is?" Bryce asked, looking more than a little pleased with himself.

She shook her head.

"Our anniversary."

"No, it's not. We've only been married—"

"It's been six months since the day I walked into the bookstore. Which, if you'll recall, was the first day you saw me naked."

"Ah yes," she said. "How could I forget?"

He held up the olives. "I thought a commemorative session was in order."

She licked her lips. "I'm supposed to open the store."

"You're the co-owner," he countered. "You can do whatever you want."

Laughing, she put her hands on her hips. "That's

hardly a good business practice, professor. Blowing off a business obligation to have sex.''

''Maybe not,'' he agreed, slipping a hand inside her robe and easing it off one shoulder. ''But it's awfully appealing.''

She shivered. She couldn't argue with that.

''Besides, I called Ronnie. She's all set to cover you.''

At that, Joan's smiled broadened. ''Well, in that case...'' She untied the sash on her robe and let it fall off her shoulders, pooling around her hips on the mattress. ''Is this what you meant by naked?'' she asked, plucking a single olive from the jar and sliding it between her lips.

''Something like that,'' he said. He reached back, then slid a slim package out from under his pillow. ''A little present,'' he said passing it to her.

She took it, then leaned over to press a kiss to his lips. ''I love you, Mr. Worthington.''

He stroked her hair, then returned the kiss—soft and sweet with the promise of so much more to come. ''I love you, too, Mrs. Worthington.'' He nodded toward the gift. ''See what you think.''

She peeled the wrapping off, smiling when she saw the present—a single copy of *The Pleasures of a Young Woman.* She opened the book to a page in the middle, her eyes skimming the text. ''Sweetheart,'' she said, meeting Bryce's eyes, ''I know just what to do with this.''

HARLEQUIN BLAZE COVER MODEL SEARCH CONTEST 3569 OFFICIAL RULES
NO PURCHASE NECESSARY TO ENTER

1. To enter, submit two (2) 4" x 6" photographs of a boyfriend or spouse (who must be 18 years of age or older) taken no later than three (3) months from the time of entry: a close-up, waist up, shirtless photograph; and a fully clothed, full-length photograph, then, tell us, in 100 words or fewer, why he should be a Harlequin Blaze cover model and how he is romantic. Your complete "entry" must include: (i) your essay, (ii) the Official Entry Form and Publicity Release Form printed below completed and signed by you (as "Entrant"), (iii) the photographs (with your hand-written name, address and phone number, and your model's name, address and phone number on the back of each photograph), and (iv) the Publicity Release Form and Photograph Representation Form printed below completed and signed by your model (as "Model"), and should be sent via first-class mail to either: Harlequin Blaze Cover Model Search Contest 3569, P.O. Box 9069, Buffalo, NY, 14269-9069, or Harlequin Blaze Cover Model Search Contest 3569, P.O. Box 637, Fort Erie, Ontario L2A 5X3. All submissions must be in English and be received no later than September 30, 2003. Limit: one entry per person, household or organization. **Purchase or acceptance of a product offer does not improve your chances of winning.** All entry requirements must be strictly adhered to for eligibility and to ensure fairness among entries.

2. Ten (10) Finalist submissions (photographs and essays) will be selected by a panel of judges consisting of members of the Harlequin editorial, marketing and public relations staff, as well as a representative from Elite Model Management (Toronto) Inc., based on the following criteria:

Aptness/Appropriateness of submitted photographs for a Harlequin Blaze cover—70%
Originality of Essay—20%
Sincerity of Essay—10%

In the event of a tie, duplicate finalists will be selected. The photographs submitted by finalists will be posted on the Harlequin website no later than November 15, 2003 (at www.blazecovermodel.com), and viewers may vote, in rank order, on their favorite(s) to assist in the panel of judges' final determination of the Grand Prize and Runner-up winning entries based on the above judging criteria. All decisions of the judges are final.

3. All entries become the property of Harlequin Enterprises Ltd. and none will be returned. Any entry may be used for future promotional purposes. Elite Model Management (Toronto) Inc. and/or its partners, subsidiaries and affiliates operating as "Elite Model Management" will have access to all entries including all personal information, and may contact any Entrant and/or Model in its sole discretion for their own business purposes. Harlequin and Elite Model Management (Toronto) Inc. are separate entities with no legal association or partnership whatsoever having no power to bind or obligate the other or create any expressed or implied obligation or responsibility on behalf of the other, such that Harlequin shall not be responsible in any way for any acts or omissions of Elite Model Management (Toronto) Inc. or its partners, subsidiaries and affiliates in connection with the Contest or otherwise and Elite Model Management shall not be responsible in any way for any acts or omissions of Harlequin or its partners, subsidiaries and affiliates in connection with the contest or otherwise.

4. All Entrants and Models must be residents of the U.S. or Canada, be 18 years of age or older, and have no prior criminal convictions. The contest is not open to any Model that is a professional model and/or actor in any capacity at the time of the entry. Contest void wherever prohibited by law; all applicable laws and regulations apply. Any litigation within the Province of Quebec regarding the conduct or organization of a publicity contest may be submitted to the Régie des alcools, des courses et des jeux for a ruling, and any litigation regarding the awarding of a prize may be submitted to the Régie only for the purpose of helping the parties reach a settlement. Employees and immediate family members of Harlequin Enterprises Ltd., D.L. Blair, Inc., Elite Model Management (Toronto) Inc. and their parents, affiliates, subsidiaries and all other agencies, entities and persons connected with the use, marketing or conduct of this Contest are not eligible to enter. Acceptance of any prize offered constitutes permission to use Entrants' and Models' names, essay submissions, photographs or other likenesses for the purposes of advertising, trade, publication and promotion on behalf of Harlequin Enterprises Ltd., its parent, affiliates, subsidiaries, assigns and other authorized entities involved in the judging and promotion of the contest without further compensation to any Entrant or Model, unless prohibited by law.

5. Finalists will be determined no later than October 30, 2003. Prize Winners will be determined no later than January 31, 2004. Grand Prize Winners (consisting of winning Entrant and Model) will be required to sign and return Affidavit of Eligibility/Release of Liability and Model Release forms within thirty (30) days of notification. Non-compliance with this requirement and within the specified time period will result in disqualification and an alternate will be selected. Any prize notification returned as undeliverable will result in the awarding of the prize to an alternate set of winners. All travelers (or parent/legal guardian of a minor) must execute the Affidavit of Eligibility/Release of Liability prior to ticketing and must possess required travel documents (e.g. valid photo ID) where applicable. Travel dates specified by Sponsor but no later than May 30, 2004.

6. Prizes: One (1) Grand Prize—the opportunity for the Model to appear on the cover of a paperback book from the Harlequin Blaze series, and a 3 day/2 night trip for two (Entrant and Model) to New York, NY for the photo shoot of Model which includes round-trip coach air transportation from the commercial airport nearest the winning Entrant's home to New York, NY, (or, in lieu of air transportation, $100 cash payable to Entrant and Model, if the winning Entrant's home is within 250 miles of New York, NY), hotel accommodations (double occupancy) at the Plaza Hotel and $500 cash spending money payable to Entrant and Model, (approximate prize value: $8,000), and one (1) Runner-up Prize of
cash payable to Entrant and Model for a romantic dinner for two (approximate prize value: $200). Prizes are valued
Prizes consist of only those items listed as part of the prize. No substitution of prize(s) permitted by
warded jointly to the Entrant and Model of the winning entries, and are not severable - prizes
or transferred. Any change to the Entrant and/or Model of the winning entries will
vill be selected. Taxes on prize are the sole responsibility of winners. Any and
described as part of the prize are the sole responsibility of winners. Harlequin
r parents, affiliates, and subsidiaries are not responsible for errors in printing of
responsibility is assumed for lost, stolen, late, illegible, incomplete, inaccurate,
ted mail or entries. In the event of printing or other errors which may result in
of prizes, all affected game pieces or entries shall be null and void.

or winners' list (available after March 31, 2004), send a self-addressed, stamped
Model Search Contest 3569 Winners, P.O. Box 4200, Blair, NE 68009-4200, or
vw.blazecovermodel.com).

terprises Ltd., P.O. Box 9042, Buffalo, NY 14269-9042.

HBCVRMODEL1

HBCVRMODEL2